KU-067-611

1000 FACTS ON
MYTHS AND LEGENDS

First published by Bardfield Press in 2004
Copyright © 2004 Miles Kelly Publishing Ltd

Bardfield Press is an imprint of
Miles Kelly Publishing Ltd
Bardfield Centre, Great Bardfield
Essex, CM7 4SL

2 4 6 8 10 9 7 5 3 1

Editor
Kate Miles

Art Director
Debbie Meekcoms

Design Assistant
Tom Slemmings

Picture Research
Liberty Newton

Production
Estela Boulton

British Library Cataloguing-in-Publication Data
A catalogue record for this book is available from the British Library

ISBN 1-84236-398-0

Printed in China

www.mileskelly.net
info@mileskelly.net

1000 FACTS ON
MYTHS AND LEGENDS

BARDFIELD
PRESS

Contents

Key

 Creation mythology

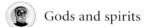 Gods and spirits

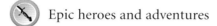 Epic heroes and adventures

Magical creatures

Life and love

Destruction and death

4

Contents

Contents

 Mothers and matriarchies 140; Trees of life 142; Fertility mythology 144; Babies and children 146; Tales of beauty 148; Stories of strength 150; Old age and long life 152; Legendary partnerships 154; Learning and knowledge 156; Tragic love stories 158; Living happily ever after 160; Tales of inspiration and courage 162; Stories of fire 164; Friendship with animals 166; Eternal life 168; Health and healing 170

Struggle with fate 172; Warnings and curses 174; Wrath and punishment 176; Flood mythology 178; How evil and death entered the world 180; Legendary 'baddies' 182; Burial beliefs 184; Underworlds 186; Pictures of paradise 188; Pharaohs and pyramids 190; Descent into the realm of the dead 192; Vampire mythology 194; Doom, death and disappearance 196; Defeating death 198; Ghosts and ghouls 200; Spirit journeys 202; Past and new lives 204; Visions of the end 206

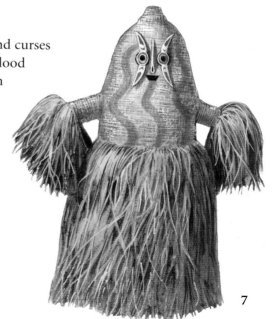

According to the Ancient Greeks

- **We know about Greek mythology** from works of art and writings from as early as 800BC.

- **The earliest Ancient Greeks**, Bronze Age farmers, worshipped a Mother Earth goddess called Gaea.

- **Myths say** that Gaea emerged out of an emptiness called Chaos.

- **Gaea gave birth** to Ourea (Mountains), Pontus (Sea) and Uranus (Father Sky).

- **The next rulers** were the children of Gaea and Uranus: 12 immortals called the Titans.

- **The children** of two Titans, Oceanus and Tethys, lived as spirits called nymphs in all the springs, rivers and seas of the world.

▲ *In early Greek artworks, the Sphynx is a monster with a man's head, a lion's body and wings. Later artworks picture the Sphynx with a woman's head and chest.*

- **Another two Titans**, Cronus and Rhea, had children who overthrew them. These were the next immortal rulers: the Greek gods and goddesses.

- **Three Greek gods** divided the universe between them: Zeus ruled the earth, Poseidon ruled the seas, Hades ruled the underworld kingdoms of the dead.

- **Some myths** say that the most intelligent Titan, Prometheus, created the first man out of clay and water.

- **Other myths** say that the chief god, Zeus, has created five races of human beings. The Gold Race lived in harmony with the gods and died peacefully. The Silver Race were quarrelsome and disrespectful, so Zeus wiped them out. The Bronze Race loved weapons and war, so brought death upon themselves. The Race of Heroes were so noble that Zeus took them to live on islands of the blessed. The Race of Iron is our own. Myths predict that we show no respect for the earth we live on, so Zeus will destroy us.

◀ *The Greeks built impressive temples to Zeus and their other gods and goddesses. You can see the ruins of many of them in the Greek islands today.*

9

Scandinavian stories

- **Norse mythology** comes from people who lived in Scandinavia in the Bronze Age. These were the ancestors of the Vikings.

- **Myths say** that in the beginning was a huge emptiness called Ginnungagap. A fiery southern land called Muspellheim first came into existence, then a freezing northern land called Niflheim.

- **The fires eventually** began to melt the ice, and the dripping waters formed into the first being: a wicked Frost Giant named Ymir. More Frost Giants were formed from Ymir's sweat.

- **The next being** that grew from the thawed ice was a cow called Audhumla. Audhumla licked an ice block into a male being called Buri.

- **Buri's grandchildren** were the first three Norse gods: Odin, Vili and Ve. They killed Ymir and threw his body into Ginnungagap. His flesh, blood, bones, hair, skull and brains became the earth, seas, mountains, forests, sky and clouds.

- **Dwarves came into** existence before human beings. They grew from maggots in Ymir's flesh.

- **Odin, Vili and Ve** created the first man, Ask, from an ash tree and the first woman, Embla, from an elm tree. The gods gave humans a world called Midgard.

- **The gods tried** to keep the evil giants away by giving them a separate land, Jotunheim.

- **The gods built** themselves a heavenly homeland called Asgard.

- **A rainbow bridge** links the realm of the gods to the world of humans. The god Heimdall was set as watchman to make sure only gods and goddesses could cross.

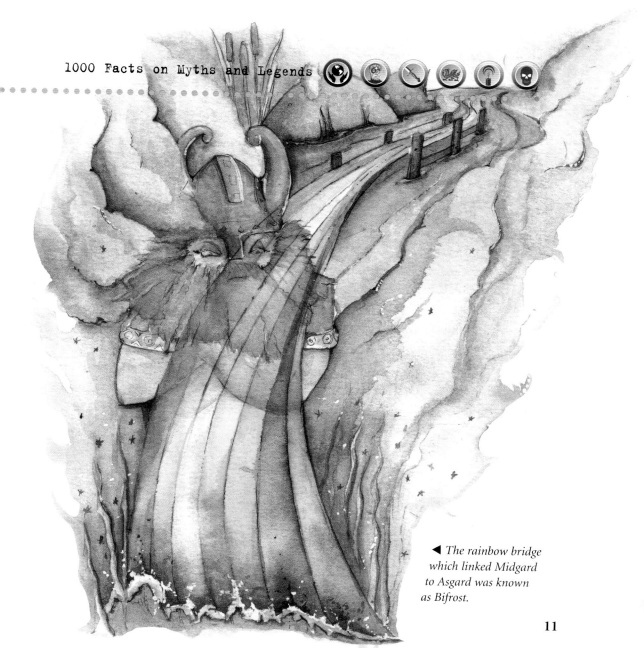

◀ *The rainbow bridge which linked Midgard to Asgard was known as Bifrost.*

Mesopotamia

- **Myths from the Middle East** are the oldest recorded mythology in the world, dating from 2500BC.

- **The Babylonian creation** myth grew from the Sumerian creation myth. It is called the Enuma Elish.

- **The Enuma Elish** was found written in a language called cuneiform on seven clay tablets by archaeologists excavating Nineveh in AD1845.

- **The Enuma Elish** says that in the beginning the universe was made of salt waters (Mother Tiamat), sweet waters, (Father Apsu), and a mist (their son Mummu).

- **The waters gave birth** to new young rebellious gods who overthrew Apsu and Mummu.

- **Tiamat and her** followers (led by a god called Kingu) were conquered by a male Babylonian god, Marduk, in a battle of powerful magic.

- **The Babylonians** pictured Marduk with four eyes and four ears, so he could see and hear everything. Fire spurted from his mouth and haloes blazed from his head.

- **Marduk became** the new ruler. He made Tiamat's body into the earth and sky. He appointed gods to rule the heavens, the earth and the air in between.

- **Human beings** were created out of Kingu's blood. Marduk made them build a temple to himself and the other gods at Babylon.

▶ *Around 2100BC, the Sumerians of Mesopotamia built massive stepped temples of mud-bricks called ziggurats.*

● **Every spring**, Babylon was in danger of devastating flooding from the mighty rivers Tigris and Euphrates. Historians believe that the Enuma Elish might have been acted as a pantomime to please Marduk so he kept order and prevented the flooding.

Ancient Egyptians

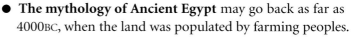

- **The mythology of Ancient Egypt** may go back as far as 4000BC, when the land was populated by farming peoples.

- **Folk in each area of Egypt** originally worshipped their own gods. Their stories spread and merged, so there are many versions and some gods are known in different forms.

- **Egyptian myths** say that in the beginning the universe was filled with dark waters.

- **The first god was Ra-Atum.** He appeared from the waters as the land of Egypt appears every year out of the flood waters of the Nile.

- **Ra-Atum spat** and the spittle turned into the gods Shu (air) and Tefnut (moisture).

- **Humans were created** one day when Shu and Tefnut wandered into the dark wastes and got lost. Ra-Atum sent his eye to find them. When they were reunited, Ra-Atum's tears of joy turned into people.

- **The world was created** when Shu and Tefnut gave birth to two children: Nut – the sky, and Geb – the Earth.

◀ *Here the sun god is holding an ankh in his right hand. This is the sign of life and the key to the Underworld.*

● **Ancient Egyptians believed** that Ra-Atum originally lived in the world with humans. When he grew old, humans tried to rebel against him. Ra then went to live in the sky.

● **Egyptian myths** were written down in hieroglyphic writing. This was invented around 3000BC, when Upper Egypt and Lower Egypt united into one kingdom.

● **It was not until** the 1820s that experts worked out what hieroglyphs meant. Before that, we knew about Ancient Egyptian mythology from old writings in other languages.

◄ ► *Hieroglyph means 'sacred carving'. Each picture stands for an object or an idea or a sound.*

South Pacific stories

- **The remote islands of the South Pacific**, such as Polynesia, Hawaii and Tahiti, were untouched by the rest of the world for thousands of years. Mythological beliefs remain strong there to this day.

- **European explorers took over many islands** in the nineteenth century. Some islanders believed that this was because they had failed to keep myths and rituals alive properly, so they started to write them down for future generations.

- **Myths from west Polynesia** say that in the beginning the creator god Tangaroa lived in a dark emptiness called Po.

- **Some stories say that Tangaroa** formed the world by throwing down rocks into the watery wastes.

- **Some myths say that Tangaroa** created humans when he made a leafy vine to give his messenger-bird, Tuli, some shade – the leaves were people.

- **Other Polynesian myths** say that the world was created by the joining of Ao (light) and Po (darkness).

- **In New Zealand**, the two forces who joined together in creation were Earth Mother and Sky Father – Papa and Rangi.

◀ *The powerful god Tangaroa is an important figure in the mythologies of many South Pacific islands.*

▲ *The beautiful island of French Polynesia. The South Pacific islands cover an area over twice the size of the United Kingdom (England, Scotland, Wales and Northern Ireland).*

- **According to stories from New Zealand**, Tangaroa was the father of fish and reptiles.

- **Other gods in myths from New Zealand are**: Haumia, father of plants; Rongo, father of crops; Tane, father of forests; Tawhiri, god of storm; Tu, father of humans.

- **Myths say that certain gods were more important** than others. These 'chief gods' vary from island to island, according to who the islanders believe they were descended from.

Aboriginal beliefs

- **The mythology** of Australia comes from wandering tribes of people collectively called Aborigines. Historians believe that they are descended from survivors of the Stone Age.
- **The creation mythology** of the Aborigines is called the Dreamtime.
- **There are various** Dreamtime stories, which came from different tribes.
- **Most Dreamtime mythology** says that in the beginning, the earth was just a dark plain.
- **Aborigines from central Australia** believed that their ancestors slept beneath the Earth, with the Sun, the Moon and the stars. Eventually the ancestors woke up and wandered about the Earth in the shapes of humans, animals and plants, shaping the landscape.
- **Myths from** central Australia say that people were carved out of animals and plants by their ancestors who then went back to sleep in rocks, trees or underground – where they are to this day.
- **Aborigines from** south eastern Australia believed heroes from the sky shaped the world and created people.

◀ *Aborigines believe that their ancestors had magical powers of creation.*

- **Tribes from the northeast** believed that everything was created by two female ancestors who came across the sea from the Land of the Dead.

- **A wise rainbow snake** plays an important part in many Dreamtime myths.

- **Aborigines believe** that even the harshest landscape is sacred because the life of the ancestors runs through it.

▶ *This Aboriginal artwork shows a monster called a Bunyip, much feared by children.*

Native Americans

- **Native American myths** come from the first people to live in North America. They walked there from Asia around 15,000 years ago when the two continents were linked by ice.

- **Native Americans** settled in many different tribes. Each tribe had its own myths and legends, although they shared many beliefs. The stories were passed down through generations by word of mouth.

- **Most tribes believed** that everything is part of one harmonious creation. Harming anything upsets the balance of the world.

- **The Iroquois** believed that Mother Earth fell into a lake from a land beyond the sky. The animals helped create the Sun, the Moon and stars.

- **According to the Algonquian,** the Earth was created by Michabo the Great Hare, from a grain of sand from the bottom of the ocean.

- **The Maidu tribe believed** that the gods Kodoyanpe and Coyote floated on the surface of a vast expanse of water and one day decided to create the world.

- **The Navajo people** believed that the first man and woman were created when four gods ordered the winds to blow life into two ears of corn.

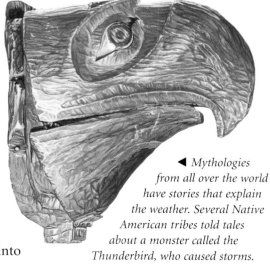

◀ *Mythologies from all over the world have stories that explain the weather. Several Native American tribes told tales about a monster called the Thunderbird, who caused storms.*

▲ *The Iroquois tribe lived in an eastern area of North America now known as New York State.*

- **Many Native American** myths say that when the world was created, humans and animals lived together.

- **Some Native American** tribes believed that all creation is ruled over by a supreme spirit.

- **In 1855**, Henry Wadsworth Longfellow wrote an epic poem called *The Song of Hiawatha*, about a real Native American hero. Many aspects of his myth differ from reality. For instance, in the poem, Hiawatha is Iroquois, when in reality he was Algonquian.

Who were the Celts?

- **After the Roman invasion** of Britain in the first century AD, the Celts were a people who lived mainly in Ireland, Scotland, Wales, Cornwall and northern France.

- **Celtic myths** were told as stories by poets called bards and priests called druids. Christian monks later wrote down the tales.

- **In Celtic creation** mythology, Ireland existed at the beginning of time and was the whole world.

- **According to** Celtic myth, the first people to settle in Ireland all died in a great flood.

- **The second race** of settlers were male and female gods called the Partholons. They fought off a race of invading monsters called the Formorians, before being wiped out by a plague.

▼ *The Celts made tools, weapons, armour and jewellery from many different metals, decorated skilfully in intricate, flowing patterns. This heavy, twisted neckband is called a torque.*

- **Another race of gods** called the Nemedians then settled in Ireland, but were forced out by Formorian attacks.

- **Tribes called the Fir Bolgs** then invaded. These were humans who knew magic.

- **A wise, skilled race** of god-like people called the Tuatha De Danaan arrived and defeated the Fir Bolgs and the Formorians.

- **Finally, a race of humans** called the Children of Mil invaded Ireland. They became the ancestors of the Celts.

- **When the Children of Mil** settled in Ireland, the Tuatha De Danaan used their magic powers to vanish from human sight, but have stayed in Ireland to this day.

▶ *Celtic tribes across Britain and Northern Europe worshipped a fearsome horned god who hunted human souls. One name for him was Cernunnos.*

23

Indian myths

▲ *The continuous interaction between the different linguistic, religious and social groups through the ages has resulted in a rich variety of Indian mythology.*

- **People have lived in India** for thousands of years. Myths are still an important part of their culture and religions today.

- **The earliest Indians** were farmers who thought that Prithivi, the Earth, and Dyaus, the sky, were the parents of all gods and humans.

- **A warrior race called the Aryans** then invaded India. They believed a god called Varuna created the world by picturing everything in his eye, the Sun.

- **Aryans believed that the storm god** Indra later took over as chief god, supported by human beings. He rearranged the universe by organizing the heavens and the seasons.

▲ *The creator god Brahma is shown looking in all directions with four heads, to show that he has knowledge of all things.*

- **The Hindu religion grew** from Aryan beliefs. Hindus believe that one great spirit is in everything. This is Brahman, whom they worship as thousands of different gods.

- **The god who creates the world** is Brahma. He emerges from a lotus flower floating on the floodwaters of chaos and thinks everything into being.

- **The god Vishnu preserves** the balance of good and evil in the universe by being born on earth as a human from time to time, to help men and women.

- **The god Shiva** is the destroyer god. He combats demons and keeps the universe moving by dancing.

- **After each 1000 Great Ages,** Shiva destroys the world by fire and flood. He preserves the seeds of all life in a golden egg, which Brahma breaks open to begin the rebirth of creation.

FASCINATING FACT
Hindu mythology says the world is created, destroyed and re-created in cycles that go on for ever.

Chinese myths

- **The Chinese myths we know** may not be the oldest Chinese stories. Certain emperors in the past burned many ancient books and also ordered traditional tales to be rewritten in line with their own religious beliefs.

- **There are many Chinese creation myths**. The most common story says that in the beginning, the universe was an egg containing a mass of chaos.

- **Most myths say** that the first being was a dwarf-like creature called Panku, who pushed open the egg. The chaos separated into a heavy mass of Earth and a light mass of sky.

- **Many Chinese people today believe** that everything in the universe has the force of one of these first two masses: Yin (the female, negative force of the Earth) and Yang (the male, positive force of the sky).

- **Myths say that Panku grew and grew** every day for 18,000 years, pushing the sky and Earth apart.

- **Some stories say that Panku then fell asleep and died**. Everything in the world was born from his body.

- **Other stories say that Panku remained alive** and carved everything in the world, with the help of a tortoise, phoenix, unicorn and dragon.

- **According to an ancient writing** called the Shu Ching, eight rulers created the universe together. These were the Three Sovereigns and the Five Emperors.

- **Many legends explain** that it is the duty of the ruler of China to keep order and balance in the universe by establishing systems of government in heaven as well as on Earth.

▶ *According to many Chinese creation myths, a creature called Panku played a vital role in shaping the world.*

...FASCINATING FACT...
Certain myths tell that the first people were created from
wet clay by a mother goddess called Nugua.

27

Early Japanese myths

- **The earliest people to** live in Japan were called the Ainu. They believed that in the beginning the world was a swampy mixture of water and earth where nothing lived.

- **According to Ainu myth**, a creator god called Kamui sent a water wagtail to the swamp. This fluttered its wings and and tail, and islands appeared from the water.

- **The Ainu believed that people** and animals were created by Kamui to live on the islands.

- **During the second and first** centuries BC people from Asia arrived in Japan. They brought a nature religion called Shinto with them.

- **According to Shinto myths** the world was at first an ocean of chaos, which gradually divided into light heavens above and heavy Earth below.

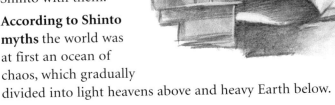

◀ *In the religion of Shinto, priests make offerings to the spirits of nature.*

- **Shinto mythology says** that the first god was like a reed shoot that grew in the space between heaven and Earth.

- **Shinto beliefs say that a female god** called Izanami and a male god called Izanagi gave shape to the world. They stood on the rainbow and Izanagi stirred the ocean with a spear. An island formed, and the two gods left heaven to go and live on it.

- **The Shinto creation myth** says that Japan was formed when Izanami gave birth to eight children who became islands.

- **Izanami and Izanagi** had many other children. These were the gods which shaped and then lived in every aspect of nature: the winds, seas, rivers, trees and mountains.

- **The ruler of the universe** is the sun goddess, Amaterasu. She was born from Izanagi's left eye.

◀ *The Shinto religion has traditional dances which date from AD400. They are performed to religious chanting and accompanied by the rhythmic beating of huge drums.*

29

Tales from Africa

◀ *Animals feature prominently in African culture. The chameleon, with its highly developed ability to change colour, lives in the trees of African forests.*

- **Numerous** tribal groups have lived in Africa for thousands of years, all with their own different myths and legends, although many shared beliefs.

- **Most African tribes believe** in one supreme creator god (who judges people wisely) and many minor gods.

- **Many myths say** that the creator god grew weary of constant demands from people, so he left the Earth and went to live in heaven.

- **The Yoruba people** of Nigeria believed that in the beginning the universe consisted of the sky, ruled by the chief god Olorun, and a watery marshland, ruled by the goddess Olokun.

- **The Yoruba believed** that a god called Obatala shaped the Earth with the help of magic gifts from other gods.

> ...FASCINATING FACT...
> Different tribal names for the creator god
> include Mulungu, Leza, Amma and Nyambe.

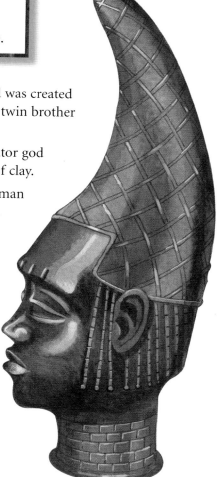

- **The Fon people** of Benin believed that the world was created by twin gods: the moon goddess Mawu and her twin brother Lisa, the Sun.

- **The Dogon people** of Mali believed that the creator god moulded the Sun, Moon, Earth and people out of clay.

- **The Pygmies believed** that the first man and woman were brought forth by a chameleon who released them from a tree in a gush of water.

- **The Yoruba believed** that the chief god, Olorun, breathed life into the first people, who were modelled from mud.

▶ *The Fon people of Benin, where this sculpture comes from, were known from the early 17th century for their skill in battle. Male warriors fought alongside a female army.*

South American stories

- **Most South American myths** we know come from the Inca race, who built a great empire in Peru from the thirteenth century AD until they were conquered by Spanish invaders in 1532.

- **Inca means 'children of the sun'.** Some South American myths say that the sun was created on an island in Lake Titicaca.

- **Inca mythology grew from ancient tales** told by tribal peoples who had lived in Peru from around 2500BC.

- **A pre-Inca Tiahuanaco myth** tells that in the beginning a god called Con Ticci Viracocha emerged out of nothingness and created everything.

- **Con Ticci Viracocha** is said to have later returned to earth out of Lake Titicaca, destroyed his world in a huge flood, and created everything again.

◀ *This statue was created by the Tiahuanaco people of Peru. This important civilization lived in the highlands around Lake Titicaca before the Incas invaded.*

- **Another myth tells how the first humans were created** by a boneless man called Con, who was the son of the sun. He was later overthrown by another child of the sun, Pachacamac, who created a new race of people.

- **An ancient coastal tribe in Peru** believed in a creator god called Coniraya. They believed he had filled the sea with fish and taught them how to farm the land.

- **The Canaris tribe believed they were descended** from an ancient parrot or macaw, who had bred with the few survivors of a terrible flood.

- **The Inca believe they magically appeared** one day from a place called Paccari-tambo, which means 'inn of origin'.

- **Myths say that the first Incas were led by eight royal gods:** four brothers and four sisters.

▼ *These modern-day Peruvians are fishing on Lake Titicaca – an important site in Inca myth.*

Who were the Maya?

- **The Maya were a great race** who lived in modern-day Guatemala, Honduras and Yucatan, around 500BC–AD1524 (when they were conquered by Spanish invaders).

- **The Mayan creation story** is written in an ancient document called the Popol Vuh.

- **The Maya believed that in the beginning** there was nothing but darkness, with sky above and sea below.

- **Myths say that a group of gods** together shaped the landscape and formed animals and birds.

- **The Popol Vuh explains** that the first two human races made by the Creators were not good enough and had to be destroyed. The first people were mindless, made from clay. The second people were soulless, made from wood.

- **The first successful people** were made out of corn, at the suggestion of a jaguar, a coyote, a crow and a parrot.

- **The Maya believe that the third race** of humans were so perfect they were almost as good as the Creators themselves. So the Creators clouded the intelligence of the humans so they could no longer see the gods.

- **The Maya believed that they could** get back in touch with the gods by taking certain mind-altering drugs.

- **The Maya believed that when human beings** were created all the world was still in darkness. People begged for some light, so that is why the Creators made the Sun, Moon and stars.

▲ *The Maya built huge stone temples and palaces in the shape of pyramids, like this one at Teotihuacan.*

```
...FASCINATING FACT...
As in the Christian creation story in the Bible, the Popol
Vuh says that women were created after men.
```

Toltec and Aztec tales

- **The Toltecs were** a great civilization in Mexico between AD900 and 1200. The Aztecs were a race of warriors who came to power in 1376. Their first ruler claimed to be a descendant of the chief Toltec god, and they adopted Toltec myths and legends.

- **The Toltecs built huge pyramid** temples which still stand, covered in pictures telling their myths.

- **We know about Aztec myths** from an ancient Aztec calendar, and a document which explains how Aztec gods fit into the calendar.

- **The Toltecs and Aztecs** believed that both humans and the gods needed to make sacrifices in order to keep the universe alive.

- **In the beginning**, the gods created and destroyed four worlds one after another, because humans did not make enough sacrifices.

- **In order to create a sun** for the fifth world, two gods sacrificed themselves by jumping into a flaming bonfire.

◀ *The name Quetzalcoatl means 'feathered serpent'. His statue is found carved into many ancient sites in Central America.*

36

- **At first the fifth world** consisted only of water with a female monster goddess floating in it, eating everything. The mighty gods Quetzalcoatl and Tezcatlipoca ripped the goddess apart and turned her body into the earth and the heavens.

- **The Aztecs believed that the sun** god and the earth monster needed sacrifices of human blood and hearts in order to remain fertile and alive.

- **Human beings were created** by Quetzalcoatl, from the powdered bones of his dead father and his own blood.

- **Quetzalcoatl and Tezcatlipoca** brought musicians and singers from the House of the Sun down to Earth. From then on, every living thing could create its own kind of music.

▲ *These Toltec ruins, known today as El Castillo, date from the eleventh century* AD.

Beliefs from Persia

- **We know many of Persia's myths** and legends from a document called the Shah name or Book of Kings. This was written by a poet called Firdausi around AD1000.

- **An Ancient Persian myth** says that in the beginning there was a flat mass of earth and water. Then evil came crashing through the sky, stirring up the landscape.

- **According to early myth**, Persia was at the centre of the world. The mighty Mount Alburz grew for 800 years until its peak touched the heavens. At its base was a gateway to hell.

- **The earliest Persian gods** were good and evil forces of nature, such as Vayu (the wind god who brought life-giving rain) and Apaosha (the demon of drought).

- **Much of Persia's mythology** comes from a religion founded by a prophet called Zoroaster in the sixth century BC. The chief god was called Ahura Mazda. His most beautiful form was the sun.

- **According to Zoroastrianism**, the world began when Ahura Mazda created time. He gave birth to everything that is good: light, love, justice and peace.

- **The first human** was a man called Gayomart. Ahura Mazda created him from light.

- **Evil entered the universe** when Ahura Mazda's jealous twin, Ahriman, attacked the world and set free hunger, pain, disease and death to spoil creation.

> ...FASCINATING FACT...
> Persia is the ancient name for modern-day Iran.

● **Ahriman killed Gayomart**, but Ahura Mazda created a new human couple, Mashya and Mashyoi. Ahura Mazda left them free to worship either himself or the wicked Ahriman as humans have been free to do ever since.

◀ *The people of Persia followed the teachings of the prophet Zoroaster, shown in the top right of this painting, from the sixth century* BC *until the country became Muslim in the seventh century.*

Greek and Roman pantheons

- **The Greek gods and goddesses** have very human qualities. They act because of love, hate and jealousy, just as we do.

- **Myths say that giants called the Cyclops** gave Zeus the gift of thunder and lightning, and Poseidon the gift of a fishing spear called a trident, with which he could stir up sea-storms, tidal waves and earthquakes.

- **The gods were believed to have taught human** beings life-skills: Zeus – justice, Poseidon – ship-building, Hestia – home-making, and Demeter – farming.

- **The gods** (except for Artemis, the hunter goddess) opposed human sacrifice and cannibalism. Zeus once punished King Lycaon for eating human flesh by turning him into a wolf.

▶ *The most famous Cyclops was named Geryon. He and his giant friends liked to feast on human flesh.*

- **The Greek gods and goddesses** sometimes fell in love with humans. Their children were heroes, such as Heracles and Perseus.

- **The gods and goddesses of Ancient Greece** were adopted by the Romans, under new names. Hence Zeus became Jove, Hera became Juno, Poseidon became Neptune and so on.

- **The stories about Greek and Roman gods**, spirits and heroes are known as Classical mythology.

- **The Ancient Greeks and Romans** believed that spirits called dryads lived inside trees.

- **In Latin, the language of the Romans**, 'templum' means the space where a shrine to a god was erected. This is where we get our word temple from.

- **Greeks and Romans would sometimes** leave small offerings at the shrine of a god. These could be food, flowers, money or sweet-smelling incense.

▶ *The Greek sea god Poseidon, whose Roman name is Neptune, held a trident with which he could stir up waves into terrible sea-storms.*

The Titans

- **The Titans were 12 immortals** in Greek and Roman mythology.

- **The strongest of the Titans** was Atlas – he held up the sky. The cleverest was Prometheus.

- **A Titan called Epimetheus** is said to have married the first mortal woman, Pandora.

- **The Titan Helios became god of the Sun.** Selene became goddess of the Moon.

- **Oceanus became god of the river** that the Greeks believed surrounded the Earth.

- **Themis became goddess** of prophecies at a city called Delphi.

- **Rhea became** an earth goddess.

- **A prophecy said** that the youngest Titan, Cronus, would be overthrown by his own son. So when Cronus's children were born, he ate them. However, his wife hid one child away – this was Zeus.

◀ *The wise Titan Prometheus helped the human race by teaching mortals special skills.*

- **When Zeus was grown up**, he fed Cronus a cup of poison which caused him to vomit up all the other children he had swallowed. These emerged as the fully grown gods and goddesses: Poseidon, Hades, Hera, Demeter and Hestia.

- **Zeus and his brothers** and sisters fought against the Titans for ten years. The Titans were finally overthrown when the gods and goddesses secured the help of the Hundred-handed Giants and Cyclopes.

- **The Titans were hurled** into an underworld realm of punishment called Tartarus. There, they were bound in chains for ever.

▶ *After the war between the gods and the Titans, the god Zeus punished the Titan Atlas by commanding him to hold up the skies on his shoulders.*

43

Norse warrior gods

- **Ancient Norse peoples** told stories about a race of gods and goddesses called the Aesir. They were brave warriors, just like the Vikings themselves, with similar feelings and fears.

- **Odin, the chief of the warrior gods**, has a high throne called Lidskialf, from which he can see anything happening in the universe.

▶ *Norse stories said that the thunder god, Thor, raced across the heavens in a chariot pulled by two enormous, vicious goats.*

▶ *Norse stories are the mythology of the Vikings –*
seafaring warriors from Norway, Sweden and
Denmark who invaded other parts of Europe.

- **The Norse gods** do not take much notice of humans. They are more concerned with battling giants and dealing with other magical creatures.

- **Odin occasionally** likes to disguise himself as a traveller and wander undetected through the world of humans – almost like taking a holiday.

- **Norse gods and goddesses** are not immortal. They can be killed by cunning magic or simple bravery, just like humans.

- **The most important warrior** goddesses are Odin's wife, Frigg (a mother goddess with fertility powers) and the beautiful Freya (goddess of love).

- **The daughters of Odin** were beautiful spirits called Valkyries. They flew over battlefields and took warriors who had died bravely to live happily in a place in Asgard called Valhalla.

- **Two days of the week** are named after Norse warrior gods. Wednesday means Woden's Day – Woden was another name for Odin, the father of the gods. Thursday means Thor's Day, after the Norse god of thunder.

- **The Aesir once fought** against gods and goddesses called the Vanir (or 'shining ones'). They finally made a peaceful alliance against the giants.

- **The ruler of the Vanir** was the fertility god Njord, ruler of the winds and the sea.

Native American spirits

- **Many Native Americans** believed they could trace their families back through legends to a particular animal or bird. They made carvings (totems) of these creatures, to help them contact the spirits of their ancestors.

- **Many tribes believed** that they would be punished by the animal spirits of their ancestors if they hunted or fished for more food than they needed.

▼ *European settlers in North America fought Native American tribes for their land. By 1890, the tribes had all been pushed onto few and far-between reservations.*

- **Four sky spirits were** important to the Pawnee: the North Star (their creator), the Morning Star (their protector), the South Star (the underworld leader of enemy forces), and the Evening Star (bringer of darkness).

- **Central tribes believed that** Sedna was the Old Woman of the Sea. She controlled sea creatures and caused storms.

- **Stories of the Algonquian** tribe say that all things in nature which are helpful to humans were the idea of a god called Gluskap. All hostile, poisonous natural things are the work of his brother, Malsum.

- **South Eastern tribes** including the Cherokee built earth mounds in the shape of sacred animal spirits, around which all tribal ceremonies were held.

- **The Arikara people of the plains** believed that the Corn Mother taught them agriculture and that they could keep peace by making offerings of smoke to the Sky Spirit.

- **Shamans or 'medicine men'** were holy men who knew how to contact spirits. They sometimes used herbs and chanting to sink into a trance, allowing a spirit to enter them and speak.

- **In the late nineteenth century** many Native American tribes performed ghost dances to ask the spirits of their animal ancestors to drive European settlers from their lands.

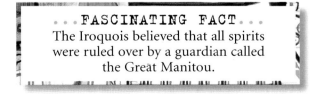

...FASCINATING FACT...
The Iroquois believed that all spirits were ruled over by a guardian called the Great Manitou.

▶ *Native Americans carved pictures of the spirits of their ancestors into whole tree trunks, known today as totem poles.*

The gods of Egypt

- **The mighty sun god**, Ra-Atum, was called many different names by Ancient Egyptians.

- **The sun god was sometimes pictured** as a scarab beetle. This is because a scarab beetle rolls a ball of dung before it, as the ball of the Sun rolls across the sky.

- **Myths say that the sun god** has a secret name, known only to himself, which was the key to all his power.

▲ *The blue scarab beetle Khephri is one of the many forms of the sun god. This amulet was made over 3000 years ago.*

- **The Ancient Egyptians believed** that part of the spirit of a god could live on Earth in the body of an animal. This is why their gods are pictured as humans with animal heads.

- **Hathor or Sekhmet** was the daughter and wife of Ra-Atum. She could take on the form of a terrifying lioness or cobra to attack and punish enemies of the sun god.

- **Osiris was the son of Ra-Atum**. He became king of Egypt and later, ruler of the underworld Kingdom of the Dead.

- **Osiris's brother, Seth**, represented evil in the universe. He hatched a wicked plot to murder Osiris and take the crown of Egypt for himself.

- **Osiris's sister and wife** was called Isis. She was a powerful mother goddess of fertility.

- **Horus was Osiris's son.** He inherited the throne of Egypt. Ancient Egyptians believed that all pharaohs were descended from Horus, and therefore they were gods.

- **An amulet is a piece of jewellery** with magical powers. Many amulets were in the shape of an eye – either the sun god's or Horus's. The sacred eye was thought to have healing powers and to ward off evil.

◄ *This picture shows the god Osiris on his throne. He wears the crown of Egypt, as does his son, Horus, who faces him. The goddess Isis is standing behind Osiris.*

Hindu deities

- **Hindus believe that one day** in the life of the supreme spirit, Brahman, is equivalent to 4320 million years on earth.

- **Hindus believe that there is a set**, correct way for everyone to behave, according to their role in society. Myths say that the god Vishnu established this code of good behaviour on earth, known as 'dharma'.

- **The wife of the mighty destroyer god**, Shiva, is a very important goddess. She has three forms: the gentle Parvati, the brave demon-fighter Durga, and bloodthirsty Kali.

- **Ganesha is the popular Hindu god** of wisdom. He is pictured with an elephant's head.

- **The Hindu word for temple is 'mandir'**. Worship is 'puja'.

- **Hindus believe that gods and goddesses** are actually present in their shrines and temples. The picture or statue that represents the god or goddess living there is known as a murti.

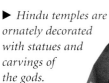

▶ *Hindu temples are ornately decorated with statues and carvings of the gods.*

- **When Hindus worship at a shrine** or temple, they leave the god or goddess a small offering of food or flowers.

- **In Hindu art, gods and goddesses** are often painted blue – the Hindu colour of holiness.

- **Hindu gods and goddesses** are often pictured with several heads or arms, to show their special characteristics. For instance, Vishnu has four arms, two holding objects which show his holiness, and two holding weapons which show his power.

- **In 1995, thousands of people in India** reported that statues of Hindu gods were drinking milk. Some people believed this was a miracle. Others said that the statues were made of porous stone which was soaking up the liquid.

▲ *The magnificent Hindu temple of Angkor Wat was built in Cambodia in the twelfth century, by the then-ruler of the Khmer empire, King Suryavarman II.*

51

Chinese divinities

- **For thousands of years,** the Chinese have worshipped the spirits of dead ancestors, believing they can help the living.

- **The first emperors** in China ruled over warrior tribes and belonged to a family called the Shang dynasty (around 1500–1050BC). They were believed to be gods, as were all following emperors.

- **According to many myths,** the first Shang emperor is the most powerful of all Chinese gods. He is known as the Jade Emperor.

- **The Jade emperor's wife** was a goddess who grew Peaches of Immortality in her palace gardens. They only ripened once every 6000 years.

- **The first Chinese man to die** and find his way to the Underworld became the chief god of the dead, Yen-Lo Wang.

- **The Chinese believe that their homes** are guarded by special spirits. Tsao Chun is the god of the kitchen. He reports on each family to heaven.

▲ *Chinese emperors kept the vast country cut off from the rest of the world until the nineteenth century.*

- **As in other civilizations,** through the centuries many real Chinese heroes have been turned into the larger-than-life characters of myths and legends. The heroes were often appointed to be gods, thousands of years after their deaths.

▲ *The Ming dynasty of emperors (AD1368–1644) built a huge palace in Beijing that ordinary Chinese people were not allowed to enter. It became known as the Forbidden City.*

- **Kuan Ti lived in the third century** AD and became famous as one of China's finest warriors. He was made a war god, to defend China from enemies.

- **Wen Chang was an outstanding** student who lived in the third or fourth century AD. He was made god of literature.

- **Wen Chang has an assistant god**, Kuei Hsing, whom people pray to for help in exams. Stories say that he was once a very gifted scholar, but incredibly ugly!

Immortals of Japan

- **The myths of the early Japanese** do not tell of a supreme spirit. Instead, they suggest that a divine force flows through all nature in the form of millions of gods.

- **The storm god Raiden** got his name from two Japanese words: 'rai' for thunder and 'den' for lightning.

- **Susano was the god of seas and oceans.** He was banished from heaven and sent to live in the Underworld.

- **Inari was the god of crops.** He is pictured as a bearded man holding sheaves of rice and riding on a fox – his servant and messenger.

▲ *Masks of spirits, demons and gods are used in a form of Japanese theatre called Noh. It is influenced by traditional stories from the Buddhist and Shinto religions.*

▶ *The religion of Buddhism spread to Japan from India. Worshippers follow the teachings of the Buddha, or 'enlightened one'.*

- **Over the centuries**, the number of nature gods increased as warrior heroes, religious leaders and emperors became gods too.

- **In the sixth century**, a religion called Buddhism was introduced into Japan and a pantheon of Japanese Buddhist gods and goddesses developed.

- **In Japanese Buddhism**, Amida is the god of a paradise for the dead. He has two helpers, Kwannon, the goddess of mercy, and Shishi, the lord of might.

- **Japanese myth says that there are about 500** immortal men and women called Sennin who live in the mountains. They can fly and work powerful magic.

- **A Shishi is a spirit pictured** as a cross between a dog and a lion (a character which came originally from Chinese mythology). It is believed to ward off evil demons, and Shishi statues are sometimes found at the entrance to temples and houses.

- **There are seven Japanese gods of luck** called Shichi Fukujin, meaning 'seven happiness beings'.

The Persian pantheon

- **The earliest Persians** worshipped nature deities such as Tishtrya, god of fertility, and Anahita, goddess of the lakes and oceans.

- **Three famous priests** of the nature god cult were the Magi – the three wise men or kings who visited baby Jesus.

- **In ancient times**, the god of victory, Verethragna, was worshipped widely through the Persian empire by soldiers. Like the Hindu god Vishnu, he was born ten times on Earth to fight demons. He took different animal and human forms.

▶ *One Persian myth says that the god Mithras brought fertility to the world by killing a bull, which contained all the strength of the Earth, and sprinkling its blood over the land.*

- **The human heroes** of Persian myths and legends were also worshipped as god-like rulers. One was the hero Faridun, who battled a monster of evil and imprisoned him at the ends of the Earth.

- **In the first and second century**, the god of light, Mithras, became an important deity. He was another warrior hero who protected creation by killing forces of evil.

- **From the sixth century**, the beliefs of a prophet called Zoroaster spread through Persia. In this religion, Zoroastrianism, the ancient gods became saints called Yazatas.

- **The chief god in Zoroastrianism**, Ahura Mazda, was later known as Ohrmazd.

- **Ahura Mazda was said to be Zoroaster's** father. Zoroaster's mother was believed to be a virgin, like Jesus's mother, Mary.

- **According to Zoroaster**, creation is protected by seven spirit guardians known as Amesha Spentas.

- **Zoroastrians believe that everyone** is looked after by a guardian spirit, or Fravashi. These spirits represent the good in people and help those who ask.

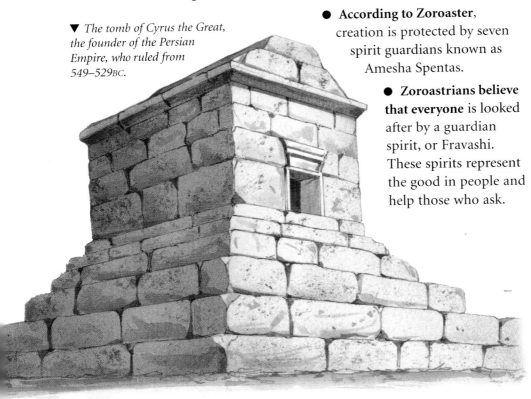

▼ *The tomb of Cyrus the Great, the founder of the Persian Empire, who ruled from 549–529BC.*

57

Celtic religion

- **Centuries before Christianity**, the Celtic peoples of the Great Britain, Ireland and Northern France, were led in worship of their gods by priests called Druids.

- **The name 'Druid' comes from** the Celtic word 'druidh', which is connected with the Greek word for oak, 'drus'. The oak was a sacred symbol and Druids held their ceremonies in oak groves.

- **Celts in different places called their gods** different names and worshipped them in different forms.

▼ *Around 2000BC early Celts built a circle of enormous stones on Salisbury Plain in England. Some historians think it may have been used for worshipping the sun. It is known today as Stonehenge.*

▶ *The leafy face of the nature god known today simply as the Green Man is found carved into old buildings across Europe.*

- **Many myths tell of a horned god** who leads a terrifying wild hunt across the sky. Some call him Herne.

- **An important race of gods** and goddesses, the Tuatha De Danann, had a mighty chief called the Dagda. He was the lord of magic, knowledge, the weather and fire.

- **Another great leader** of the Tuatha De Danann was the warrior god Nuada. He had a magic sword which conquered all his enemies.

- **The hero Lugh was master of all skills** – including magic. After many mighty deeds, he became an immortal.

- **Three important goddesses** are concerned with battle and death: the cruel Morrigan; the goddess of Ulster, Macha; and Badb, who sometimes took the form of a raven.

- **A Celtic god known today as 'the Green Man'** was carved into early Christian churches across the British Isles and Europe. He represented the power of nature, which died and was reborn each year.

- **In England, traditional Morris dances** re-enact Celtic springtime celebrations. Morris men leap into the air as a symbol of life triumphing over death.

Sacrifices for gods

- **The Maya used to play** a ball-game a bit like football. Historians think that at the end of the match, one side was sacrificed to the gods – but they do not know whether it was the winners or the losers!

- **The first wife** of the Hindu god Shiva was Sati. Sati's father tried to disgrace Shiva, and in protest, Sati sacrificed herself by throwing herself onto a sacred fire.

- **The chief Norse god, Odin**, demanded that warriors did not just give themselves up to death fearlessly, but that they actually welcomed death, in his honour.

- **The ancient Hindu fire god**, Agni, had seven tongues to lick up sacrifices of butter burnt on a sacred fire.

- **A Bible story** tells how God asked Abraham to offer him his only son, Isaac, as a sacrifice. God stopped Abraham just in time, once he had tested his obedience.

- **A sacred fire** to the Roman goddess Vesta was tended by specially chosen girls called the Vestal Virgins. They had to sacrifice ever having a boyfriend or getting married.

- **In Native American tribes**, dancers wearing 'false face masks' to ward off evil spirits often made offerings of food and 'corn animals' to the good spirits in nature.

▲ *The Maya had a ball-game in which players used their elbows, hips and knees to hit the ball. A similar game is still played in Central America today.*

- **Thousands of people** were sacrificed at a time to the Aztec sun god Huitzilopochtli, who demanded plentiful offerings of human hearts.

- **The Romans** often offered the deaths of gladiators to honour a particular god or goddess.

- **Druid priests** sometimes made sacrifices to the Celtic gods by hanging up criminals or prisoners of war in big wicker cages and burning them alive.

▲ *The wealthy backer of a Roman gladiatorial games often dedicated the deaths of the gladiators to his or her favourite god or goddess.*

Gifts from gods

▲ *The French heroine Joan of Arc was made a saint by the Catholic church 500 years after she had been burned at the stake for witchcraft and lying against God.*

- **In Greek myth,** when Perseus went to kill the Gorgon, the gods gave him a helmet of invisibility, winged sandals, and a highly polished bronze shield – with a clue to use it as a mirror.

- **According to Egyptian** myth, the god Osiris taught people the skill of farming and gave them laws and religious rites.

- **A French story** says that Joan of Arc heard a voice from God telling her to go into an ancient church and dig behind the altar. She found a great sword which had been used in holy wars called the Crusades, which no one knew had been buried there.

- **In Greek myth**, the goddess Athena gave a hero called Bellerophon a golden bridle with which he could catch the magical winged horse, Pegasus.

- **A Japanese myth** says that when the sun goddess, Amaterasu, was hiding in a cave, the other gods enticed her to come out with the gift of the first ever mirror.

- **Inuit myths** tell how it was the raven who brought many gifts to humans.

▲ *Greedy King Midas won the gift of 'the golden touch' – but ended up begging the gods to take it back.*

- **In Greek myth**, the goddess Thetis knew her hero son, Achilles, would die in the Trojan Wars. She tried to protect him with armour made by the gods' blacksmith, Hephaestus. She failed.

- **A Christian story says** that when Jesus was on his way to die on the cross, a woman called Veronica wiped his bleeding face. The imprint of Jesus's features was left on her handkerchief.

- **A Greek myth says** that King Midas asked the gods for 'the golden touch'– anything he touched was turned into gold. He soon regretted the gift when he tried to eat and drink .

- **The *Ramayana* tells how the great god Indra** gave the monkey hero Hanuman the power to choose his own death, as a gift for helping Prince Rama.

Making mischief

- **In Native American myths**, the trickster god Coyote is usually up to no good. However, he sometimes uses his cunning to help the human race, for example, by getting rid of giants.

- **The Polynesian god Maui** is one of the greatest mischief-makers in all mythologies. Like Coyote, he too sometimes uses his tricks to help humans.

- **Kobolds were a type of earth-spirit** or dwarf said to live in German silver mines. They enjoyed causing trouble for human miners, such as explosions and rockfalls.

- **The Aborigines of Arnhem Land** in the Northern Territory of Australia believe in rock spirits called Mimi. The Mimi can be kind and helpful to humans, but if strangers disturb them, they cause severe illnesses as punishments.

- **Stories from the Caribbean** tell of a fun-loving half-man, half-spider character called Anansi. He loves to create havoc for his arch-enemy, Tiger.

▶ *There are many amusing Afro-Caribbean traditional tales about a cunning spider character called Anansi.*

> **· · ·FASCINATING FACT· · ·**
> Loki was a famous trickster in Norse mythology who enjoyed
> stirring up trouble between the gods and the giants.

- **Japanese mythology is filled** with ghost stories. The spirits of the dead often cause trouble for those who hurt them while they were alive.

- **Some people believe that the power** of the great Celtic god Lug dwindled away over the centuries until he became a mischievous sprite called a 'lugh-chromain' or leprechaun.

- **In Eastern European myth**, a kikimora is a female house spirit. If the household is kept dirty and untidy, the kikimora will whine, whistle and tickle the children at night.

- **In World War II**, fighter pilots and plane engineers blamed trouble-making sprites called Gremlins for anything that went wrong with their aircraft.

▶ *Every leprechaun is believed to have a secret stash of hidden gold.*

Tricks played on gods

- **Native American Algonquian** myth says that the god Gluskap thought he was so great that there was no one in the universe who would not obey him. A woman defeated his boast by bringing him her baby – which of course would not listen to a word he said!

- **The Egyptian goddess Isis** created a poisonous snake to bite the sun god. Isis said she would only cure him if he told her his secret name – so giving her all his power.

- **In Norse mythology**, prophecies said that a mighty wolf called Fenris would kill the chief god, Odin. The gods found a way to trick Fenris into being tied up with a rope made of strong magic.

- **The Tupinamba people** of South America once thought that a great shaman, Maira-Monan, was growing too powerful. They killed him by tricking him into walking into a fire of powerful magic.

- **Osiris, the great God of Egypt**, was secretly murdered in a trick by his jealous brother, Seth. Under false pretences Seth coaxed Osiris into a coffin, then he slammed the lid shut so Osiris suffocated.

- **According to Greek myth**, the Titan Prometheus tricked the chief god Zeus into accepting just animal bones and fat from humans as sacrifices. Ever since, humans have been allowed to keep the tasty meat for themselves.

- **A Native American myth** tells how the god Coyote tried to smoke a rabbit out of his burrow. The rabbit turned the trick, by hurling the fire out at the god!

- **In Chinese myth**, the Jade Emperor once gave Monkey the job of Keeper of the Heavenly Horse. This sounded like an important honour, but in fact, Monkey was just a stable boy!

- **According to myths** from the South Pacific islands, the god Maui tried to trick a goddess called Hina into granting immortality to the world. The furious Hina crushed Maui to death.

- **Norse myth says that the blind god** Hodur was tricked into killing his twin brother Baldur, who was loved by all creation. This was the beginning of the end for the warrior gods.

▲ *The Egyptian goddess Isis knew such powerful magic that she once tricked the great sun god, Ra-Atum.*

67

The oral tradition

- **Myths and legends existed** in civilizations all over the world for thousands of years before writing was developed. They were told as entertainment by professional poets specially trained to remember the long works and perform them out loud. This is called the oral tradition of literature.

- **An epic is an adventure story** in the form of a long poem, which follows the brave deeds of a human hero as he struggles against magical dangers.

- **The heroes of many epics** are often born into royalty and brought up away from their parents.

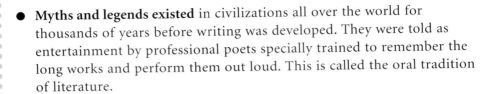

▼ *One of the enduring Greek stories is of Daedalus, whose son Icarus flew too close to the sun, melting the wax on the wings that had been crafted for him to escape from King Minos.*

- **Many epic heroes** possess superhuman powers and are helped by gods or spirits.

- **Most epic heroes** possess at least one magical weapon or object with magic powers.

- **Epic poetry provided** early peoples with standards and goals for how to live a good life.

▶ *The crews of these Ancient Greek triremes sailed off to do battle with ships and lands taking with them their stories of legends and myths.*

- **The most famous epics** are the Greek poems *The Iliad* and *The Odyssey*. Some historians think these were written by a blind man called Homer around 750BC. Others think they were composed gradually in the oral tradition by a series of poets.

- **Archaeologists have found** written fragments of *The Iliad* and *The Odyssey* dating from the fourth century BC. However, the oldest complete manuscripts are dated from the tenth century AD.

- **Medieval poets were called bards** or troubadors. They often chanted their tales to music.

> ···FASCINATING FACT···
> The name for traditional storytellers in some parts of Africa was griots.

69

Gilgamesh

- **This epic poem is from Sumeria** – one of the earliest civilizations to have city states, laws and irrigation.

- **Gilgamesh was a real king** of the Sumerian city Uruk, around 2700–2500BC.

- **In the poem, King Gilgamesh** is a man of mighty strength who is loved dearly by the gods.

- **When the nobles of Uruk** complain to the gods that King Gilgamesh is a tyrant, the Mother Goddess makes a hero called Enkidu to challenge him. Gilgamesh meets his match in Enkidu, and the two become firm friends.

- **When Enkidu dies**, Gilgamesh begins to fear his own death. He embarks on a quest to find out how to become immortal.

- **Gilgamesh does not win eternal life**, but is rewarded with a plant which will keep him young and strong for the rest of his days. When a watersnake steals it from him, he nearly despairs.

- **Gilgamesh finally realizes** that the only type of immortality humans can achieve is fame through performing great deeds and building lasting monuments.

- **The poem was discovered in 1845**, when archaeologists were excavating at the ancient city of Nineveh.

- **Experts think that** *Gilgamesh* was first written down on clay tablets in an ancient language called cuneiform. It is the earliest recorded major work of literature.

- **Fragments of** *Gilgamesh* have been found by archaeologists in ancient sites throughout many countries of the Middle East.

▲ *This ancient Sumerian stone relief shows the hero Gilgamesh as the central figure.*

Heracles's labours

- **Heracles was Zeus's son** by a mortal woman. Zeus's divine wife, Hera, was so jealous that she would only allow Zeus to make Heracles immortal if Heracles could complete a series of impossible tasks.

- **Unlike other Greek heroes**, Heracles does not set out seeking fame, fortune and immortality. He only performs the labours because it is commanded by the gods.

- **Two labours involved killing** terrifying beasts: the man-eating Nemean lion and a nine-headed, poisonous swamp monster called the Hydra.

- **Four labours involved** capturing magical creatures alive: the golden deer sacred to the goddess Artemis, the vicious Erymanthian boar, a ferocious bull belonging to the god Poseidon, and some flesh-eating horses.

- **One labour was to get rid** of a flock of birds who shot their feathers like arrows at people.

▲ *An Ancient Greek statue of the formidable father god, Zeus.*

- **Two labours involved stealing** precious objects: the belt of the fearsome Amazon queen, Hippolyte, and a herd of cattle belonging to the giant, Geryon.

- **A humiliating labour was** to clean out the biggest, dirtiest stables in the world.

- **The final labours required** journeying to the ends of the Earth to fetch some golden apples and venturing into the Underworld to bring back the three-headed guard dog, Cerberus.

- **After many further adventures**, Heracles was finally poisoned. As he lay dying, Zeus took him up to Mount Olympus, at last to join the gods as an immortal.

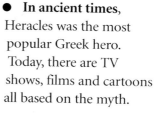

- **In ancient times**, Heracles was the most popular Greek hero. Today, there are TV shows, films and cartoons all based on the myth.

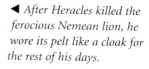

◀ *After Heracles killed the ferocious Nemean lion, he wore its pelt like a cloak for the rest of his days.*

Jason and the Argonauts

- **According to Ancient Greek** myth, Jason was a prince of Iolcus who was exiled from his home as a child when his uncle seized the throne.

- **A wise centaur called Chiron** brought up Jason with other abandoned future heroes, including the mighty warriors Achilles and Aeneas.

- **It was the centaur**, Chiron, who gave Jason his name. It means 'healer'.

- **Jason returned** to Iolchus to claim his throne. His uncle agreed to give up the throne if Jason travelled to the ends of the earth and brought back a magical Golden Fleece.

- **Jason built a huge ship** for the voyage, called the *Argo*. The goddess Athene gave a magic bough for the prow, which was able to speak words of advice.

- **The greatest heroes** in Greek mythology, including Heracles, volunteered to help Jason in his task. They became known as the Argonauts.

- **Jason and the Argonauts** faced peril after peril on their sea voyage. Many of these were reworked later into the epic poem, *The Odyssey*.

- **A beautiful witch-girl** called Medea fell in love with Jason. She used her magic to help Jason win the Golden Fleece from its owner and escape. It belonged to the king of Colchis – her own father.

- **The name Medea** means 'cunning'.

- **Jason later left Medea**, breaking an oath to the gods. This brought trouble upon him. Some said that Medea murdered him in revenge. Others believed that he died an old beggar man.

▲ *One hazard encountered by Jason and the Argonauts on their voyage was the Symplegades. These were rocks which clashed together, crushing ships passing between them.*

Theseus's adventures

- **There are many myths** about a hero called Theseus who became king of Attica in Greece. Historians have proved that a real King Theseus did once exist.

- **According to legends,** Theseus was the secret son of a king called Aegeus. Theseus was brought up away from Attica, to keep him safe from enemies who wanted the throne for themselves.

- **As a young man,** Theseus travelled to Attica to claim his birthright. He chose a long route through many dangers, because he wanted to prove himself on the way.

- **Theseus once took** a mighty bronze-plated club from a thug who tried to kill him. He used the weapon for the rest of his life.

- **Theseus liked to punish criminals** by their own evil methods. One villain liked to tie people between two bent young trees which sprang back and ripped them apart. Thanks to Theseus, he got a dose of his own medicine.

- **When Theseus reached Attica,** his father's new wife tried to poison him. Luckily King Aegeus recognized his son just in time.

◄ *Myth says that the Minotaur was created when the god Poseidon cruelly caused King Minos's wife to fall in love with a magnificent bull. Their affair resulted in a child with a human body and a bull's head.*

▲ *A perfect example of Doric architcture, a temple to the goddess of Athens, Athene, was built in 447BC. Today it is called the Parthenon.*

- **Each year, Aegeus** had to send young people as a human sacrifice to King Minos of Crete. Brave Thesesus volunteered to go. He was thrown into a maze called the Labyrinth to be eaten by a ferocious bull-headed man, the Minotaur. Instead, Theseus slew the monster.

- **King Minos's daughter**, Ariadne, fell in love with Theseus and helped him to escape from the Labyrinth.

- **Archaeologists have found** that the ancient royal palace of Crete was laid out rather like a maze, and that a dangerous sport a bit like bull-fighting was very popular. The myth of the Minotaur might have arisen from stories about them.

- **Historians credit Theseus** with building Athens as an important Greek centre of power. Today it is the capital of the country.

The Trojan War

- *The Iliad* **is an epic poem** which tells of events at the end of a ten-year war between the Ancient Greeks and the Trojans.

- **The Trojan War** began when a Trojan nobleman called Paris kidnapped Helen, Queen of Sparta. Her father asked the Greeks to help win her back.

- **When *The Iliad* was composed**, no written records about the Trojan War existed. The story comes from information passed down by word of mouth for hundreds of years.

- **The city of Troy definitely existed**, as archaeologists have discovered its remains. The city burned in 1184BC.

- **The principal characters** in *The Iliad* are the courageous noblemen of both sides. They aim to win fame by fighting honourably and dying a glorious warrior's death.

◀ *The Trojan War ended when Greek warriors secretly entered the city of Troy by hiding inside a huge wooden horse.*

● **The greatest Greek warrior** is Achilles. When he argues with the Greek commander, Agamemnon, and withdraws from battle, the Greek army suffers terribly.

● **The greatest Trojan warrior** is Paris's brother, Hector.

● **Goddesses and gods play a major role in** *The Iliad*. They support different sides, just as if they were football teams, giving their human favourites advice and help.

● *The Iliad* **is the earliest** written work from Ancient Greece.

● **The Greeks eventually won** the Trojan War. The hero Odysseus had the idea of building a huge wooden horse, inside which many Greek warriors hid. The Greeks left it outside the gates of Troy and the Trojans took it inside the city, thinking it was a gift. At night, the Greek warriors scrambled out and destroyed the city.

▲ *This painting on an Ancient Greek vase shows the warrior Achilles. He was protected by divine armour – except for a small spot on his heel, which is where he finally received his death wound.*

79

Odysseus and The Odyssey

- **The Odyssey is an adventure** story which follows the Greek hero, Odysseus, after the Trojan War, on his long and difficult sea voyage home.

- **Odysseus and his men** have to face many magical dangers on their journey, including monsters and giants.

- **On one occasion**, some of Odysseus's sailors eat lotus fruit, which makes them forget all about returning to their families and homes.

- **Odysseus has to sail safely** past the Sirens. These are half-woman, half-bird creatures who live on a craggy seashore. They sing a magical song that lures sailors to steer their ships onto the rocks to their deaths.

- **The goddess of war**, Athena, acts as Odysseus's patron, giving him special help and guidance.

- **The sea god Poseidon** hates Odysseus and seeks to shipwreck him.

- **By the time Odysseus finally** reaches his palace in Ithaca, he has been away for 20 years. Disguised as a beggar, only his faithful old dog recognizes him.

▲ *One Greek legend says that the Sirens were so furious when Odysseus escaped their clutches that they drowned themselves .*

...FASCINATING FACT...
Unlike its companion poem, *The Iliad*,
The Odyssey has a happy ending.

- **Once home, Odysseus's troubles** are not over. Powerful suitors are pressurizing his faithful wife, Penelope, for her hand in marriage, so they can seize Odysseus's crown.

- **Women often hold positions** of great power in the poem. For instance, Circe is a very powerful sorceress who turns some of Odysseus's sailors into pigs. The goddess Calypso keeps Odysseus captive on her island for seven years.

▶ *After 20 years at war, Odysseus returns to his kingdom disguised as a beggar. He is greeted by his old dog, who then dies content.*

The Aeneid

- ***The Aeneid* is an epic poem which follows** the adventures of a Trojan prince, Aeneas, after the end of the Trojan War.

- ***The Aeneid* was not composed** in the oral tradition. The Roman author, Virgil, wrote it down in Latin.

- **Virgil was the well-educated son** of a farmer. The Roman Emperor, Augustus Caesar, recognized his writing talent and became his patron (backed him with money).

- **Virgil based the legends** in his poem and its structure on the epics *The Iliad* and *The Odyssey*.

- **In *The Iliad*, Aeneas fights** many times against the Greeks, but is always saved by the gods because he has another destiny.

- **It was popular in the sixth century** BC to picture part of the legend of Aeneas on vases – how Aeneas carried his father to safety out of the smoking ruins of Troy.

- **Virgil designed *The Aeneid*** to give Augustus and the Roman empire a glorious history. It explains that the gods themselves instructed Aeneas to travel to Italy, to be the ancestor of a great race – the Romans. It shows how Augustus Caesar was directly descended from the mighty hero.

- **In *The Aeneid*, Aeneas falls in love** with Queen Dido of Carthage and then abandons her, sailing for Italy. Virgil probably made up this myth to explain the hatred that existed between Rome and Carthage in the third century BC.

- **Virgil began *The Aeneid*** in 29BC and worked on it for the last ten years of his life. As he lay dying of a fever, he asked for the poem to be burnt. However, Augustus Caesar overruled his wishes.

● **A great Italian poet** called Dante Alighieri (1265–1321) used Virgil's style and the legends of *The Aeneid* as the basis for his own poem, the *Divine Comedy*.

▶ *According to one Ancient source, the poet Virgil was tall and dark with the appearance of a countryman.*

Romulus and Remus

- **The story of Romulus and Remus** tells how twin boys grew up to build the foundations of the mighty city of Rome.

- **Versions of the myth were written** by many of the greatest Roman writers, such as Livy, Plutarch and Virgil.

- **According to the legend**, Romulus and Remus were descendants of the hero Aeneas. They were the sons of a princess and the war god, Mars.

- **As babies, the twin boys** were cast out by their evil great-uncle, who had stolen the king's crown from their grandfather. They survived because a she-wolf found them and let them drink her milk. A bird also fed them by placing crumbs in their mouths.

▶ *The Roman legend of Romulus and Remus may have been the inspiration for the Tarzan story. In both cases, abandoned infants were brought up by animals.*

- **When the twins grew** up they overthrew their wicked uncle, restoring their father to his rightful throne.

- **The twins built a new city** on the spot where they had been rescued by the she-wolf. However, they quarrelled about who should be ruler, and Romulus killed Remus.

- **Romulus became king** of the new city and named it Rome, after himself.

- **The new city had too many men** and not enough women. Romulus hatched a plot whereby he held a great celebration and invited neighbouring communities – then captured all their women!

- **Romulus built a strong army**, to defend Rome from attacks by local tribes. He brought about a 40-year period of peace.

- **One day, Romulus was surrounded** by a storm cloud and taken up to heaven, where he became a god.

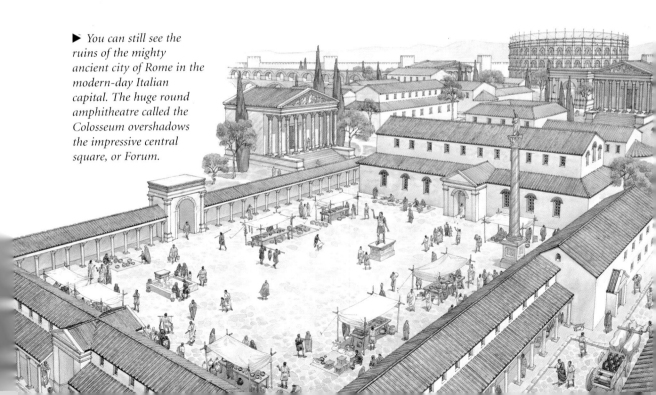

▶ *You can still see the ruins of the mighty ancient city of Rome in the modern-day Italian capital. The huge round amphitheatre called the Colosseum overshadows the impressive central square, or Forum.*

Beowulf

- **The epic poem** *Beowulf* was written in the Anglo-Saxon language by an unknown English person around AD700–750.

- **The legend focuses on the adventures** of a Viking hero, Beowulf. The action takes place in the south of Sweden and Denmark.

- **Christianity was introduced** to England around AD600. The poem blends traditional elements of Norse myth such as warrior culture and fate with belief in a Christian god.

- **Beowulf risks his own life** to help other people by battling three terrifying monsters: Grendel, Grendel's mother, and a dragon.

- **The monster Grendel** is said to bear 'the mark of Cain'. This is a reference to the Bible story in which Adam's son Cain killed his brother Abel.

- **Beowulf is fatally wounded** when all his chosen warriors desert him through fear – except for his courageous nephew Wiglaf.

- **At the end of the poem**, the dead Beowulf is laid to rest in a huge burial mound. A similarly impressive burial mound, dating around AD650, was discovered at Sutton Hoo in Suffolk in 1939.

- **The oldest manuscript** of *Beowulf* that exists today was made from an original by monks in about AD1000. Many other older copies were destroyed when King Henry VIII ordered monasteries and their libraries to be closed down in the late 1530s.

◀ *This helmet was buried along with many other treasures in a splendid longboat in the seventh century at Sutton Hoo in Suffolk, England. Historians think the treasures belonged to an important Anglo-Saxon king.*

- **The modern-day film** *The Thirteenth Knight*, starring Antonio Banderas, is based on the gripping Beowulf legend.

- **The only remaining copy** is kept in a controlled environment behind glass in the British Museum.

▼ *Beowulf has to descend to the depths of a murky lake to fight the monster Grendel's ferocious mother.*

Sigurd the Volsung

- **Different versions of the legend** of the warrior hero Sigurd the Volsung exist in Norse, British and German mythologies.

- **The earliest existing written** version appears as part of the Norse epic poem, *Beowulf*, where a storyteller recites the saga as entertainment for some warrior nobles.

- **The most detailed** version of the myth is known as *The Volsunga Saga* (written around AD1300 by an unknown author).

- **The legend is a superb adventure** story about heroic deeds, magic, love, betrayal, jealousy, danger and death.

- **Volsung is the King of Hunland**, and great-grandson of the Norse father of the gods, Odin.

- **Volsung's son, Sigmund**, is similarly mighty. In an episode which parallels the legend of the young King Arthur pulling the sword from the stone, Sigmund is the only man who can pull Odin's sword out of an oak tree trunk.

- **Odin's favourite is Sigmund's son**, the hero Sigurd. Odin helps Sigurd choose a horse that is related to his own magical steed.

◄ *The hero Sigurd and his adventures were the subject of several operas by the nineteenth-century German composer Richard Wagner.*

- **Odin's sword was smashed** when Sigmund died. Sigurd has the fragments recast into a fearsome weapon called Gram.

- **Sigurd's first quest is to find** a hoard of dwarf gold, guarded by a dragon. One of the treasures is a cursed ring. This inspired the modern-day author J R R Tolkien in his *Lord of the Rings* books and also the composer Wagner in his series of operas, *The Ring of the Nibelung*.

▶ *J R R Tolkien's* Lord of the Rings *saga, inspired by the Sigurd legend, has recently been made into three stunning movies.*

FASCINATING FACT
The saga contains an early version of the story of *Beauty and the Beast*.

King Arthur

◀ *Mont-Saint-Michel is a rocky islet off the coast of northwest France, where legend says King Arthur once slew a giant.*

- **Legends about an extraordinary** British king called Arthur have been popular for over 800 years, yet historians have never been able to prove whether he was a real figure in history.

- **If a real Arthur** did exist, he is likely to have lived much earlier than the medieval times of the legends.

- **Many authors have written** Arthurian legends over the centuries, including: the French medieval poet Chretien de Troyes, the fifteenth-century writer Sir Thomas Malory, and the Victorian poet Lord Tennyson.

- **Arthur's father was said** to be King Uther Pendragon. The name means 'dragon's head'.

▶ *King Arthur was finally killed by his own son. One legend says that his body was buried at the holy site of Glastonbury.*

- **One legend says that Arthur** slew a fearsome giant at Mont-Saint-Michel in France, then conquered the Roman Empire.

- **Many legends focus on the knights** at Arthur's court and the idea of courtly love, in which women are purer beings in God's eyes than men. A lover knight is required to obey the wishes of his lady without question or reward.

- **Arthur's knights went on many** dangerous quests to test their bravery and honour. The most difficult was a search for the Holy Grail – a goblet that caught Jesus's blood as he died on the cross. It was believed to disappear when anyone who had sinned came near it.

- **The Round Table** was first mentioned in legends written by the French medieval poet, Robert Wace, in AD1155.

- **Arthur is finally killed** by his enemy Mordred – who is in fact his own son.

- **Some legends say that King Arthur** was taken to a country of blessed souls called Avalon and will return when Britain falls into greatest danger.

Cuchulain

- **The correct way to pronounce** Cuchulain is 'Cu-hoo-lin'.

- **Cuchulain was a warrior hero** supposed to have lived in Ireland in the first century AD.

- **Stories say that Cuchulain was born** when the king of Ulster's sister was magically swept away by a god called Lug. However, the baby's name was originally Setanta.

- **Setanta was schooled by the greatest heroes** and poets at the king of Ulster's court.

- **As a teenager, Setanta killed single-handed a ferocious dog** belonging to a blacksmith called Culan. This is how he got his nickname, because Cuchulain means 'Hound of Culan'.

- **Cathbad the Druid once prophesied** that any boy who became a warrior that day would become the most famous hero in all Ireland – but would die young. Cuchulain was 15, but decided to arm himself to fulfil the prophecy. He wanted a short, glorious life rather than a longer, more unremarkable one.

- **Cuchulain was a rare thing called a 'berserk warrior'**. This means that he was possessed by a frenzy in battle. Power sparked from his hair, his body hissed with heat, his eyes bulged, his muscles stretched his skin, and blood frothed on his lips.

- **Cuchulain won his wife**, Emer, by defeating the tricks of a cunning chieftain called Forgal the Wily.

- **Cuchulain died in battle**. He had been terribly wounded, but had lashed himself to a standing stone, so he would die on his feet, fighting to the end.

- **Cathbad the Druid's prediction came true**, because in Irish mythology, Cuchulain is indeed considered to be the greatest of all Irish warrior heroes.

▶ *The Celts believed that a goddess of death called Badb often appeared at battlefields in the form of a raven. According to one legend, a raven drank from the wounded Cuchulain's streaming blood as he fought heroically to his death.*

Finn McCool

- **The legend of Finn McCool** might be based on a warrior hero who lived in Ireland in the third century AD.

- **Finn's real name was Demna**. 'Finn' was a nickname meaning 'fair haired'.

- **Finn was raised in secret** by a druidess and a wise woman, who taught him god-like powers of strength and speed.

- **Finn was very wise and just**. This is because he once ate a magical fish called the Salmon of Knowledge.

▲ *Legend says that the hero Finn McCool created the rock formation called the Giants' Causeway in Northern Ireland. In fact, it was formed when lava from a volcano cooled and set.*

- **Finn won the position of head** of the Fianna – an elite group of warriors sworn to defend the High King of Ireland. Under his leadership, the Fianna had many daring, magical adventures and rose to the height of their glory.

- **The Fianna possessed** a magic Treasure Bag which contained weapons from the gods, objects with healing powers, and Faery gifts.

- **Finn fell in love with a goddess**, Sava. She bore him a son, Oisin, who became a famous Fianna warrior and a great poet.

- **Finn once had an argument** with a giant in Scotland. They threw rocks across the sea at one another, which created a rock formation today called the Giants' Causeway.

- **Legend says that Finn** and the Fianna lived on the Hill of Allen in present-day County Kildare.

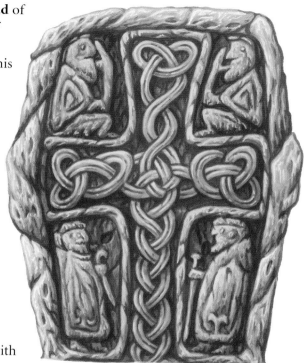

▲ *This Celtic cross shows Finn McCool with his thumb in his mouth. He is touching his magical 'tooth of knowledge', which had an extraordinary power telling him whatever he wanted to know.*

95

Kotan Utunnai

- **The epic poem *Kotan Utunnai*** belongs to a race of people from the Stone Age called the Ainu.

- **The Ainu lived on** remote Japanese islands, untouched by the outside world for hundreds of years, until other Japanese people made contact in around AD1670.

- **The Ainu were hunter-gatherers** who had no agricultural systems, no metalworking skills and no system of writing.

- **The epic *Kotan Utunnai*** was first written down by an English missionary in the 1880s.

- ***Kotan Utunnai*** is one of several Ainu epic poems which focus on wars with a people called the Okhotsk from the tenth to the sixteenth centuries.

- **Like many epic heroes**, the hero of *Kotan Utunnai* puts family loyalty above his own desires. This means he has to seek revenge for the murder of his parents.

- **In the myth, the world** of humans is strangely mixed up with the magical world of gods, spirits and demons. From time to time humans hear the sound of gods fighting like a low rumbling across the land.

- **Many human epic heroes** have god-like qualities, but the hero of *Kotan Utunnai* is so god-like that even the gods themselves sometimes find it hard to believe he is human!

- **Unlike many other epics**, there are several powerful female characters in *Kotan Utunnai*. Women have great fighting skill and are considered equal in importance with men.

- **The epic demonstrates** the Ainu belief that when you die, if you have led a good life, you will be reborn. However, if you were a wrong-doer, you will remain dead.

▶ This is an Attush coat worn by the earliest people in Japan, the Ainu. The patterns around all the openings of the coat are designed to stop evil spirits from entering.

The Ramayana

◀ Hindus believe that the hero Rama was one of the ten human forms of the god Vishnu.

- **The Indian epic poem** the *Ramayana* focuses on the battle between the forces of good and evil in the universe.

- **Historians believe that it was** largely composed between 200BC and AD200. The poet is believed to be called Valmiki, although hardly anything is known about him.

- **Like the Greek epic *The Iliad*,** the *Ramayana* involves the rescue of a stolen queen (called Sita).

- **Like the Greek epic *The Odyssey*,** the *Ramayana* follows a hero (Prince Rama) on a long and difficult journey.

- **Prince Rama's enemy** is the mighty demon, Ravana. He can work powerful magic, but is not immortal and can be killed.

- **The demon Ravana's followers** are known as Rakshasas. They can shape-shift and disguise themselves so they do not appear evil. This way, they can tempt good people to do the wrong thing.

- **The poem** demonstrates that it is important to respect animals. Rama needs the help of the hero Hanuman and his army of monkeys to rescue Sita.

- **The story says** that Rama and Sita are earthly forms of the great god Vishnu and his wife, Lakshmi.

- **Hindus see the** *Ramayana* as a book of religious teaching because Rama and Sita are models of good behaviour.

- **The legend ends** when Rama has ruled as king for 10,000 years and is taken up to heaven with his brothers.

▶ *The monkey god Hanuman was the son of the wind and a great hero who helped Prince Rama.*

Gassire's Lute

- **An African tribe called the Soninke** have an epic poem called *Gassire's Lute*. It was composed between AD300 and AD1100 as part of a group of songs called the *Dausi*.

- **Most other songs in the *Dausi*** have been forgotten.

- ***Gassire's Lute* is a tale** about the ancestors of the Soninke, a tribe of warrior horsemen called the Fasa.

- **The Fasa lived around** 500BC in a fertile area of Africa bordered by the Sahara Desert, Senegal, Sudan and the river Nile.

- **The hero of the legend**, Gassire, is a Fasa prince who longs for his father to die so he can become a famous king.

- **The heroes of other epic poems** usually put their lives at risk trying to help other people. This epic is strikingly different, because the hero puts his own desires in front of everything else.

- **Gassire realizes that all things die**, and that the only way to win lasting fame is to be remembered as a hero in battle songs.

▲ *A musician plays a lute by plucking its strings, similar to playing the guitar.*

- **Gassire has a lute made,** so he can sing of his own adventures. However, the lute will only play once it has been soaked with blood in battle.

- **Gassire leads his eight sons** and followers into war against an enemy tribe. It is only when all but one of Gassire's sons have been killed that his lute finally sings.

- **Gassire grieves for the dead**, but is filled with joy now he has a great battle song to bring him fame.

◄ *The Fasa ancestors of this Soninke woman were like medieval knights. They fought on horseback with spears and swords not just in battle but also for sport.*

Mwindo

- **The epic of *Mwindo*** belongs to the Nyanga tribe of Zaire, in Africa.

- **The poem was first written down** in 1956, when the Nyanga tribe still lived by hunting, gathering and growing their food.

- **The poem was performed** as a ritual over 12 days, to give protection from sickness and death.

- **The legend begins** when Chief Shemwindo forbids his wives to bear him any male children. Despite this, a little boy is finally born – Mwindo, which means 'first-born male'.

▲ *Master Lightning is the hero Mwindo's guardian and helper in his adventures.*

- **Shemwindo tries to kill** his son by burying him alive, then by drowning him. Baby Mwindo has superhuman powers which help him escape.

- **Mwindo overcomes his enemies** with the help of friends who include Hedgehog, Spider and Lightning.

- **Mwindo holds a magic sceptre** that he uses to perform powerful spells, such as bringing the dead back to life. He also has a magical bag of good fortune.

● **Mwindo is an example** of good behaviour. He forgives his father and makes peace. In turn, his father makes amends by sharing half of his kingdom with his son.

● **When Mwindo kills** a dragon, Lightning teaches him the lesson that humans are just a part of the universe, not the most powerful thing in it.

● **The main message of the myth** is that all forms of life should have respect for each other: the gods and creation, humans and animals, men and women, the young and the old, the healthy and the sick.

▶ *Storytelling has been a traditional method of keeping myths and legends alive in all cultures.*

Magical creatures

- **According to Chinese myth** there were five types of dragon: dragons who guarded gods, dragons who guarded emperors, dragons who controlled wind and rain, dragons which deepened rivers and seas, and dragons who guarded hidden treasure.

- **In Greek myth, a centaur** was half-man, half-horse. A satyr was half-man, half-goat.

- **The Phoenix was a magical bird** which lived for 500 years. It died by setting fire to itself, and was then born again from the ashes.

- **Sleipnir was an eight-legged horse** faster than the wind. He belonged to the chief Norse god, Odin.

- **In 1842 in America**, the famous Phineas T Barnum's travelling circus show displayed a 'real' mermaid. It turned out to be created from a monkey's body and a fish's tail!

- **In the Caribbean**, mermaids are called water-mamas. People believe that if you get hold of a water-mama's comb, she will grant you a wish.

▶ *Dragons are found in mythologies from all over the world, but play a particularly important role in traditional tales from China.*

◀ *Traditional belief in mermaids inspired Hans Christian Andersen's famous modern fairytale,* The Little Mermaid.

- **Philippine myths** tell of Alan – creatures who are half-human, half-bird. They live in forests and look after children who have lost their parents.

- **Unicorns are featured in the myths** of many civilizations. They are rare, beautiful creatures with the body of a horse and a single, spiral horn.

- **In Chinese mythology**, Hsigo are monkeys with bird-like wings.

- **In myths, salamanders** can survive in fire. Unfortunately, real salamanders are not magically fireproof.

105

Mythological monsters

- **Myths from the Aborigines** of Australia tell of a swamp monster called the Bunyip who hunts children at night.

- **In Greek mythology**, the Sphinx had a woman's face, a lion's body, and a bird's wings. It killed travellers who could not work out its riddles.

- **Many Scandinavian myths** feature hairy, cruel creatures called trolls who live inside the Earth and are expert metalworkers.

- **Greek stories said that a manticore** had a lion's body, but a human face – with three rows of teeth. It shot poisoned spines from its tail.

- **The Hound of the Baskervilles** was a monstrous dog in a book by the Victorian writer Sir Arthur Conan Doyle. The tale of the gigantic hound from hell has become a modern myth.

▶ *The most famous Sphinx statue in Egypt lies at the foot of Khafre's pyramid at Giza. Parts have been worn away over the centuries, but it would originally have looked like this.*

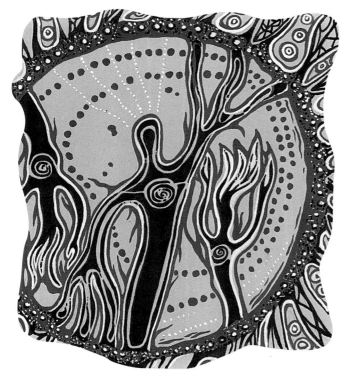

◄ *Aboriginal artwork, such as this Bunyip painting, can be found over sacred rocks and cliffs throughout tribal territories in Australia.*

● **The Norse hero Beowulf** battled a monster called Grendel. This man-eating hulk is described as a 'shadow-walker' from hell.

● **In Greek myth**, the Chimaera was a fire-breathing monster with a lion's head, a goat's body and a serpent's tail.

● **A gryphon** was a cross between a lion and an eagle, which first appeared in myths of the Middle East.

● **A basilisk or cockatrice** appears in the Bible, as well as Greek legend. It was a snake with a cockerel's wings and a dragon's tail. J K Rowling featured the monster in a *Harry Potter* story.

● **Medusa the Gorgon** was a female monster in Greek myth who had writhing snakes for hair. Anyone who looked at her face was turned to stone.

107

Modern monsters

▲ King Kong *is a classic US movie made in 1933. It featured a colossal giant gorilla.*

● **There have been thousands** of sightings of a huge sea monster in Loch Ness, Scotland, since it was first reported in AD565.

● **Strange footprints** have been found in West Africa. Stories say they belong to a dinosaur-like swamp creature called the Mokele-Mbende.

● **A huge ape-man nicknamed Bigfoot** or Sasquatch has been seen in North American forests. Two men claimed to have filmed it in 1967, but many believe the film is fake.

● **Since 1983 there have been over 600 sightings** of a big cat similar to a puma on Bodmin Moor, Cornwall – but no firm evidence that such a creature is at large.

● **The Komodo dragon** is a type of giant lizard which lives today in islands in Indonesia.

◄ *The Komodo dragon is the largest type of lizard in the world, measuring up to 3 metres long.*

- **In 1921, the first explorers of Mount Everest** claimed to have seen 'abominable snowmen' or 'Yetis'. There have been many sightings since.

- **The life story of an Englishman** called Joseph Merrick (1862–1890) gave rise to the legend of the Elephant Man. Joseph suffered from Proteus Syndrome which made him horribly disfigured.

- **Myths about werewolves** may have arisen from the illness lycanthropy. Sufferers think they are wild beasts – especially at full moon.

- **Scandinavian stories of gigantic sea monsters** called kraken may be based on real-life giant squid. These are known to have reached out and torn sailors from rafts.

- **The modern myths of Godzilla** and King Kong arose from ideas that giant-sized prehistoric creatures might emerge from secret hiding places and attack civilization.

Giants

- **The Ancient Greeks believed** that the immortals Gaea and Uranus gave birth to three one-eyed giants called the Cyclopes and three hundred-handed giants called the Hecatoncheires.

- **According to the legends of European settlers** in North America, the Grand Canyon was formed when a giant lumberjack called Paul Bunyan walked along trailing his pickaxe on the ground behind him.

- **In Celtic legend, the Formorian giant**, Balor, had an 'evil eye'. One glance killed whoever it fell upon.

- **In Norse mythology**, the giants were the sworn enemies of the gods. Their ruler was King Utgard-Loki.

- **Several passages from the Old Testament** of the Bible tell of tribes and kingdoms of giant-sized people.

▶ *The Bible story of Goliath can be found in the Book of Samuel, Chapter 1 Verse 17. The giant was from a race of people called the Philistines.*

◀ *The nineteenth-century writer Oscar Wilde wrote a famous story in which a Selfish Giant befriended a mysterious little boy, who taught him happiness.*

● **The most famous giant** in the Bible was the warrior Goliath, killed by the shepherd boy David.

● **According to the Mesopotamian** epic poem *Gilgamesh*, the home of the gods in the Cedar Forest of Lebanon was guarded by a giant called Humbaba.

● **A giant man holding a club** is carved into the hillside at Cerne Abbas in Dorset, England. No one knows who made him or why. Historians think he may date from AD185.

● **In Greek myth, Talos** was a fearsome giant made of bronze who guarded the island of Crete.

● **The tallest man on record** was an American, Robert Wadlow, who died in 1940. Even at 2.7 metres tall, he was nowhere near as tall as the giants of myths and legends.

▶ *Big, stupid, clumsy and greedy giants feature in myths and legends from many parts of the world.*

Magical possessions

- **The Chinese spirit, Monkey**, had a deadly iron fighting stick which could change magically into a tiny needle, for keeping behind his ear.

- **King Arthur wielded a mighty sword called Excalibur**, given to him by a strange spirit called the Lady of the Lake.

- **The mighty Norse thunder god, Thor, had a throwing hammer**, Mjollnir, which never missed its target, and a belt, Meginjardir, which doubled his already superhuman strength.

- **The Celtic hero Lug had a boat called *Wave-Sweeper*** that could travel over land and sea, and a sword called the Answerer that could cut through anything.

▶ *The prophet Moses used his magic staff to help the Israelites escape from slavery in Egypt. He wielded power over the Red Sea, and the pursuing Egyptian army were drowned.*

● **According to Bible stories**, the prophet Moses had a staff which God enabled to work magic, rather like a wand.

● **In the *Ramayana*, Prince Rama possessed** the god Vishnu's bow, Brahma's shining arrows, and Indra's quiver to keep them in.

● **The Norse goddess Freya** owned a spectacular dwarf-crafted necklace called the Brisingamen and also a feather-coat which gave the wearer the power of flight.

● **A Chinese legend tells** how some kind villagers helped the hero Bao Chu by using their own clothes to make him a magic coat. It kept him warm even when he fell into a river of ice.

● **The Dagda, the chief of a race of Celtic gods** called the Tuatha De Danann, had a magic cauldron which never ran out of food.

● **Greek myth** says that the god of the Underworld, Hades, owned a helmet of invisibility.

◀ *When King Arthur was dying, he ordered Sir Bedivere to throw Excalibur back into the lake it came from. A mysterious hand rose from the waters to claim it.*

Norse world order

- **Two main written sources** tell us what the Norse people believed about the universe. *The Prose Edda* is a collection of myths recorded by an Icelander called Snorri Sturluson (1179–1241). *The Poetic Edda* is a collection of 34 ancient poems recorded in the seventeenth century.

- **Many Viking carvings show pictures** of what the Norse people believed the universe to be like.

- **The Norse people thought** there were nine worlds arranged on three levels.

- **The uppermost worlds** were: Alfheim – home of the light elves; Vanaheim – home of the fertility gods; Asgard – home of the warrior gods.

- **The middle worlds** were: Midgard – home of humans; Nidavellir – home of the dwarves; Jotunheim – home of the giants; Svartalfheim – home of the dark elves.

◄ *According to Norse myth, at the end of the world the giant sea-serpent Jormungand will swim ashore to join a battle against the warrior gods.*

- **Norse myth said that a giant serpent** called Jormungand lived in the sea surrounding the middle worlds, circling them.

- **The underworlds** were: Muspellheim – a land of fire; and the freezing land of Niflheim, which included Hel – home of the dead.

- **The Norse warrior gods** kept young and strong by eating the Golden Apples of Youth belonging to a goddess called Iduna. Without these, they would face old age and death.

- **Characters from the Norse worlds** such as giants, dwarves and elves also found their way into many European fairy tales.

▲ *Norse kings had court poets who composed gripping poems about heroes and their battles. The poets performed them on long, cold winter nights as entertainment.*

···FASCINATING FACT···
Inspiration for the names in JRR Tolkien's *Lord of the Rings* trilogy came from characters in the nine Norse worlds.

115

Animals and birds

- **According to the Dogon** of Africa, animals once lived in heaven with the Creator. Humans stole a male and a female of each animal by sliding them down the rainbow.

- **Ravens have lived** at the Tower of London in England for over 1000 years. Myth says that if the birds ever leave, disaster will follow.

- **Stories brought by African slaves** to the Caribbean tell how animals and birds and humans all used to live together, speaking the same language.

- **Ancient Arab legends told** of an enormous bird called the roc. Modern scientists have since found the bones of a giant-sized bird in the swamps of Madagascar.

- **In Ancient Egypt**, cats were sacred to the goddess Bastet. When a pet cat died, the family had it mummified just like a dead human!

- **The chief Norse god** Odin had two pet ravens, Hugin and Munin. They flew through the universe and brought back news.

▲ *A mummified cat and dog from Ancient Egypt. The Ancient Egyptians believed that if they preserved a dead body from decay, its spirit could live for ever.*

- **Around 600BC**, a Greek slave called Aesop collected animal stories which had a moral message. They have become known as *Aesop's Fables*.

- **The Arikara tribe of Native Americans** believed that dogs were spirit messengers between them and their gods.

- **Rudyard Kipling's** *Just So stories* (1902) are like myths. They explain how animals came to be as they are – such as how the elephant got his trunk.

- **The Greek goddess** Athena was often pictured with an owl on her shoulder. She was the goddess of intelligence, which is why owls have traditionally been thought of as wise birds.

▶ *The tale of a plodding tortoise who beats a speedy hare in a race is one of the most famous of* Aesop's Fables.

117

Explanations of natural phenomena

▲ *The firebird is an especially important creature in the mythologies of Russia and other eastern European countries. The legends inspired a famous ballet choreographed by Fokine, to music by Stravinsky.*

- **According to Greek myth,** winter occurs because the goddess of the harvest, Demeter, grieves for six months each year when her daughter, Persephone, has to live in the Underworld.

- **Hawaiian legends say** that the bad-tempered goddess Pele lives inside the volcano Mount Kilauea, spitting out lava to turn living things into stone.

- **In Mayan mythology,** Kisin is an evil earthquake spirit. He lives under the earth with the souls of people who have killed themselves.

- **Stories from Zambia and Zimbabwe** say that a shooting star is the storm god Leza, watching over people.

- **According to the Kono people of Sierra Leone,** the creator god once gave a bat a basket of darkness to look after. The bat spilled some, which is why he flies at night – trying to catch it.

- **Some Native American myths** say that storms are created by an enormous flying creature with flashing eyes called the Thunderbird.

- **In Chinese**, the word 'dragon' also describes thunder and lightning. And tornadoes over oceans are known as 'sea dragons'.

- **According to Norse myth**, the Aurora Borealis, or Northern Lights, are the glowing beauty of a frost giantess called Gerda.

- **Many ancient civilizations** have myths which feature 'firebirds', such as the phoenix. These may have arisen from the winged shape of light that blazes around the sun during a total eclipse.

- **An Afro-Caribbean story** says that Anansi the spider-man accidentally smashed a pot containing all the common sense in the world. It was scattered on the wind and all creatures got a little bit.

▶ *The glowing lights of the Aurora Borealis can sometimes be seen in the night skies over northern countries such as Norway, Sweden and Iceland.*

Stories of the stars

▲ *Halley's Comet can be seen once every 75 or 76 years. It is featured on the eleventh-century Bayeux tapestry, which shows the conquest of England by the Normans.*

- **Western names for star constellations** come from Classical mythology, such as Orion – the hunter son of sea god Poseidon.

- **Norse myth says** that the stars were sparks that flew out of the firey land of Muspellheim, set in the sky by the gods.

- **According to European settlers in North America**, when Halley's Comet came speeding towards Earth in 1835, a hero called Davy Crockett hurled it safely back into space.

- **An ancient myth from the Dogon people** of West Africa tells of a tiny planet which takes 50 years to orbit the star Sirius. It was not discovered by Western scientists until 1862.

- **In Greek mythology**, Antiope was the mother of the evening and morning star.

120

- **The Bororo tribe of South America believe** that the stars are naughty children who climbed into the heavens to escape punishment, but became trapped there.

- **According to Inuit legend**, the Pleiades are a pack of hunting dogs who chased Nanook the Bear up into the sky.

- **Astronomy was highly advanced** in the Toltec, Aztec, Inca and Maya civilizations. The Maya calendar did not just mark a yearly cycle of days and months, but tracked complicated patterns in time over three million years!

- **In Native American mythology**, a hero called Poia who grew up with the Blackfoot tribe was the son of a star and a mortal woman.

- **Some historians think the Ancient Eygptians** built their pyramids to launch the souls of their pharaohs to particular stars. For instance, the three pyramids at Giza line up with certain stars in the constellation Orion.

◄ *The three pyramids at Giza were one of the Seven Wonders of the Ancient World. The Great Pyramid was the tallest building on Earth for nearly 4500 years, until the nineteenth century. The French general Napoleon calculated that it contained enough stone to build a wall 1 metre high around the whole of France.*

Stories of the Sun

- **The Inuit believe** that they lived in total darkness, until Raven flew to a far-off country and stole them a piece of sunlight.

- **A Chinese myth** tells that there were once ten suns who took it in turns to cross the sky. One day they all decided to appear together. The earth began to scorch, so the gods commanded an archer called Yi to shoot dead all but one.

- **The Incas sacrificed** honoured young girls to the sun god, Inti, at the June solstice (the shortest day of the year).

- **The Ancient Egyptians** believed that every day the sun god Ra-Atum sailed across the sky in a Boat of Millions of Years. At night, he made a perilous journey through the Underworld.

- **An important centre for the worship of Ra-Atum** was Heliopolis. This is Greek for 'sun city'.

- **Many Native American plains** tribes held a yearly sun dance that lasted around four days. The dancers aimed to draw the Sun's power into themselves.

- **Navajo Native Americans** believed that a god called Tsohanoai carried the Sun on his back during the day. At night, he hung it on the wall of his house.

◀ *The Sun has been worshipped in many cultures through time.*

▼ *This photo of the Blackfoot Native American tribe was taken in Alberta, 1907, at their yearly sun dance.*

- **An Indian myth** tells how the sun god, Surya, was so bright that his wife ran away to live in a shady forest.

- **Myth says that one grandson of the sun goddess** Amaterasu married the goddess of Mount Fuji, and one of their great-grandchildren became Japan's first emperor.

- **The Greek sun god Apollo** was also god of music, prophecy, archery and healing, and the protector of shepherds.

Rivers, lakes and the sea

▲ *Hindus believe that bathing in the mighty river Ganges in India can wash away their sins. When a Hindu dies, they like the ashes of their burnt dead body to be scattered on the waters.*

- **German legend says** that beautiful mermaids called Lorelei lived on rocks in the river Rhine, luring fishermen to their deaths.

- **In Greek myth**, a Triton is a sea creature like a merman who can control the waves.

- **Norse mythology says that the goddess of the sea**, Ran, owned a huge fishing net she used to catch sailors.

124

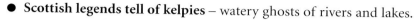

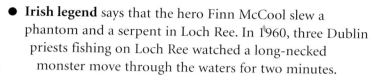

- **Scottish legends tell of kelpies** – watery ghosts of rivers and lakes.

- **Irish legend** says that the hero Finn McCool slew a phantom and a serpent in Loch Ree. In 1960, three Dublin priests fishing on Loch Ree watched a long-necked monster move through the waters for two minutes.

- **Greek myth says that the Aegean Sea** is named after King Aegeus, who drowned himself in the ocean when he was led to believe that his son, Theseus, had been killed.

- **According to Hindu myth,** the goddess Ganga lived in heaven until there was a terrible drought on Earth. Then the god Shiva helped her flow safely down into the world as the sacred river Ganges.

- **A Finnish myth says t**hat the goddess of the sea and creation, Luonnotar, was once pregnant for 730 years. She finally gave birth to a man, Vainamoinen. He swam ashore to the country that was to become Finland.

▲ *The Irish hero Finn McCool accomplished feats of amazing strength and bravery.*

- **A Persian myth tells of a hero called Keresaspa**, who battled for nine days and nights in an ocean with a monster called Gandarewa, who could swallow 12 people at once.

- **The sacred animal of the Greek sea god Poseidon was the horse**. This is perhaps why waves are sometimes described as white horses.

125

Mountains and the Moon

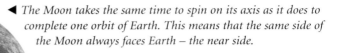

◀ *The Moon takes the same time to spin on its axis as it does to complete one orbit of Earth. This means that the same side of the Moon always faces Earth – the near side.*

● **Ancient Greeks believed that** Mount Olympus was the home of the gods. It is in northern Greece and is 2917 metres high.

● **The moon god** of the Inuit Native Americans is called Igaluk. They believe he has powers over hunting.

● **According to the Dakota Native Americans**, Hokewingla is a turtle spirit who lives in the Moon.

● **A Chinese myth** said that the Earth was square, and the heavens were supported above it by five mountains (one in each corner and one in the centre). The western mountain, K'un Lun, was the source of the Yellow River.

● **According to Finish mythology**, silver forms in the earth wherever light lands from the Moon, Kuu.

● **Babylonian myth says** that the sun god Shamash drove his chariot every evening to a mighty mountain and disappeared inside.

● **The Greek goddess of the Moon**, Selene, used magic to make a handsome shepherd called Endymion sleep for ever, so she could enjoy his beauty for eternity.

● **Before Mount Everest was renamed** after a western climber (Sir George Everest), its traditional name was Chomo-Lung Ma, which means 'Goddess Mother of the Universe'.

- **According to a Japanese myth,** the moon god, Tsukiyomi, once severely annoyed his sister the sun goddess, Amaterasu. This is why the Sun and the Moon never look each other in the face.

- **The capital city of the Inca** Empire, Machu Picchu, lies up a mountain in the Andes in Peru. At the top of the neighbouring mountain, Huayna Picchu, is an Inca temple to the Moon.

▼ *Machu Picchu, capital city of the Inca Empire, was built on a mountain more than 2280 metres above sea-level. This is almost twice as high as the highest mountain in Britain, Ben Nevis.*

Women in myth and legend

- **According to legend**, the queen of Sheba was a wealthy ruler who lived in modern-day Yemen around 900BC and took a splendid entourage to visit King Solomon of Jerusalem.

- **In Classical myth**, the Amazons were a race of female warriors who lived at the ends of the Earth.

- **The Victorian writer Tennyson** wrote a mythical poem called *The Lady of Shalott* about a woman who chose to break a curse that was upon her – even though it meant she would die.

- **Pocahontas** was a Native American born around 1595. She encouraged peace between the tribes and European settlers, and became a legend in her own lifetime.

- **Martha Cannary**, born in Missouri on 1 May 1852, braved many dangerous adventures in the 'Wild West' and became famous as the legendary 'cowgirl', Calamity Jane.

◀ *The Lady of Shalott was imprisoned in a tower. She was allowed to look at the outside world only via a mirror. If she looked directly through a window, she was cursed to die.*

▲ *The Bible story of the queen of Sheba's visit to King Solomon of Jerusalem can be found in the Book of Kings I, Chapter 10, Verses 1–13.*

- **According to the Bible**, Mary Magdalene was Jesus's closest female friend.

- **Boudicca** was a legendary queen of the Iceni tribe of Britain, from around AD25 to 61. She raised the whole of southeast England in revolt against the Romans.

- **Semiramis** was a mythical queen of Assyria who ruled Babylon, Egypt and Libya for 42 years before ascending to heaven as a dove.

- **In Greek myth**, Arachne was a woman who challenged the goddess Athena to a weaving contest. Athena turned her into a spider!

- **A heroic legend** tells of Violette Szabo, an undercover agent in German-occupied France during World War II. She was finally captured, imprisoned, tortured and executed.

Holy people and prophets

- **Legend says that the founder of Sikhism**, Guru Nanak, once disappeared into a river. Days later he emerged, saying that he had been with God.

- **According to Greek myth**, the god Apollo condemned a woman called Cassandra to the fate of prophesying truthfully, but never being believed.

- **Legend says that around** AD550 **an Indian priest** called Bodhidharma crossed the sea from China to Japan standing on a bamboo. He introduced Zen Buddhism to Japan.

- **The Druid High Priest Cathbad** was a great prophet in Celtic legend.

▲ *The Dome of the Rock is a mosque in Jerusalem built between* AD685 *and 691 by an Arab caliph.*

◀ The Japanese have traditionally loved creating beautiful water gardens and parks. Zen Buddhist gardens are designed extremely simply to encourage serenity and meditation.

● **In sixteenth-century France,** Nostradamus wrote prophecies predicting world events as far ahead as AD3500. Some people believe he foresaw the rise of Adolf Hitler and the death of Princess Diana.

● **The earliest prophet of any world religion was Zoroaster,** who was born in northeast Persia (modern-day Iran) around 1200BC.

● **According to Greek myth,** a man called Tiresias was blinded by the gods, but given the gift of prophecy to soften the blow.

● **Mother Shipton was a prophetess from North Yorkshire,** around the sixteenth century. Some people think she predicted the Great Fire of London, railways, aircraft and the Internet.

● **The Dome of the Rock in Jerusalem** was built on the spot from which legend says the Prophet Muhammad ascended into heaven.

● **Some people believe** that all the great holy leaders in history, including Jesus, Krishna and Buddha, have been manifestations of one great prophet – the Maitreya. According to an artist called Benjamin Creme, the Maitreya is alive today and living in an Asian community in the East End of London, waiting for the right time to declare himself to the world.

131

Magicians, witches and wizards

◀ Baba Yaga, an important character in eastern European legend, is a typical witch in that she flies through the air on a broomstick and has a talking cat as an assistant.

● **Stories from eastern Europe** tell of a wicked witch called Baba Yaga. Her house scuttles about on chicken's legs.

● **The magician Merlin** was King Arthur's most trusted advisor. Merlin warned Arthur that Guinevere would bring him grief – and indeed she did.

● **Sikkim is a tiny kingdom in the Himalayas** where belief in magic is still strong. A maharaja who died in 1963, Sir Tashi Namgyal, was believed to be able to control the weather.

● **Greeks and Romans** worshipped the goddess of darkness, Hecate, at crossroads. Today she is worshipped by those who practise black magic.

● **Entertainers on the Indonesian island of Bali** perform myths about a witch called Rangda. The character came from a wicked queen called Mahendradatta who lived 1000 years ago.

● **Aztec sorcerers** used black mirrors of polished obsidian to predict the future. Their patron was the god Tezcatlipoca – 'lord of the smoking mirror'.

132

- **In 1487**, James Sprenger and Henry Kramer wrote *The Malleus Maleficarum* – a book of rules for detecting witches. It was used by the church in Europe for 300 years to accuse people of black magic and condemn them to death.

- **One of the most famous wizards in myth and legend is Gandalf,** a character in J R R Tolkien's *The Lord of the Rings* stories.

- **The story goes** that in the days of Queen Elizabeth I, all the witches in Hampshire gathered to create a 'cone of power' to chase the Spanish Armada away from England. In fact, a storm did drive the fleet back to Spain – so severe that few ships arrived intact.

- **In Greek mythology**, an enchantress called Circe was the aunt of a beautiful witch-girl called Medea. They both knew powerful magic.

▶ *The most famous witch of recent times is the clever Hermione Grainger, a character in J K Rowling's* Harry Potter *stories.*

Demons and devils

- **'Devil' comes from the Hindu** word 'deva'. 'Demon' comes from the Greek word 'daemon'. The Christian word 'Satan' comes from the Hebrew word 'shatana', which means 'enemy'.

- **Some Nigerian tribes** believe they can drive away demons by summoning up the spirits of their dead ancestors through masked dances.

- **In Japanese mythology**, Oni are demons with two horns, rather like the devils in Christian stories. They wear tiger skins and fly about, hunting for the souls of evil people.

- **In myths from the Middle East**, firey demons are often known as 'djin'. These came to be known in Western myths as 'genies'.

- **The many demons in Hindu mythology** might have been inspired by the people who lived in India before the ancestors of the Hindus invaded.

▲ *The Middle Eastern legend of Alaa U'Din, or Aladdin, tells how a poor boy finds a lamp which contains a fearsome genie that can grant his wishes.*

▲ *Stone gargoyles on churches have an important practical function as well as being decorative.*

● **Gargoyles are carved stone demons** that drain water from church roofs. The name comes from a great dragon called Gargouille whom people in the seventh century believed lived in the river Seine in Paris.

● **The Christian image of the devil** probably came from pictures of the Greek nature god, Pan. Pan was half-man, half-goat, with cloven hooves and two horns.

● **The roofs of Chinese temples** were built curving upwards at the edges so that any demons falling from the sky would be swept up and away.

● **The evil Hindu demon**, Ravana, had ten heads and twenty arms. He tricked the god of creation into giving him special powers of protection, so no god or other demon could harm him.

● **In Sumerian myth**, a dreaded female demon is known as Lamashtu, or 'she who destroys'.

▼ *The curved roof of the Temple of Confucius is designed according to traditional Chinese beliefs to ward off demons. Confucius was a Chinese leader who lived from 551 to 479BC. Millions of people still follow his teachings today.*

Mysterious places of myth and legend

- **Aborigines** believe that the land is filled with spirits and sacred to their ancestors. Uluru (Ayers Rock) is one of the most holy places.

- **Stonehenge** is a circle of standing stones in Wiltshire, England, dating from around 2800BC. It might be a temple to the sun.

- **Since the 1980s**, crop circles have been appearing in wheat fields in Britain. Some say they are the work of alien visitors.

- **Over 200 ships and planes** have vanished in an area off Florida called the Bermuda Triangle. Some believe that strange energies exist here.

- **Many myths have grown up around a reported UFO crash near Roswell**, USA, in 1947. Film footage of aliens has even emerged – though this has never been proved genuine or fake.

▲ *Ancient gigantic figures on Easter Island were carved from volcanic rock and erected facing the sea.*

- **At Carnac in France,** thousands of huge stones are arranged in parallel rows. No one knows which ancient people put them there or why.

- **In 1927**, a pilot discovered enormous line drawings etched into the Nazca plains in Peru. Archaeologists think people created them 1000 to 2500 years ago, although no one knows why.

▲ *Uluru, or Ayers Rock, in central Australia is a massive lump of sandstone that rises 335 metres out of the ground.*

- **Dozens of giant stone statues stand on Easter Island in the Pacific Ocean,** probably made between AD1000 and 1500. They may represent the guardian spirits of the islanders' ancestors.

- **Some people believe that the first human moonwalk in 1969** was a myth made up by USA officials, who were determined to beat the Russians. The event could have been filmed in the Nevada desert at a location called Area 51, which remains a top secret government zone to this day.

- **Varanasi is a city in India** on the banks of the river Ganges. Hindus believe that anyone who washes in the waters will go straight to heaven when they die.

137

Lost locations

- **The Greek writer Plato** described a continent called Atlantis in the Atlantic Ocean, which suddenly vanished. Many have since tried to find its ruins and failed.

- **In the year 2000**, divers discovered the Ancient Greek city of Heraklion at the bottom of the sea near Alexandria.

- **During the sixteenth and seventeenth centuries**, many explorers to South America tried to find a mythical place rich in gold called El Dorado. No one ever found it.

- **In the 1860s**, a French explorer discovered 400 square kilometres of ninth- to thirteenth-century stone temples in the Cambodian jungle. Nearby was the twelfth-century city of Angor Thom, which rivalled Ancient Rome in size and population.

▲ *The lost city of Atlantis might perhaps have been located off the Straits of Gibraltar.*

- **Nothing remains of the famous** Hanging Gardens of Babylon (in modern-day Iraq). Stories say that Emperor Nebuchadnezzar built them for his wife, because she missed the hills of her own country, Persia.

- **On 23 August in** AD79, Mount Vesuvius in Italy erupted, burying towns for miles around. More than 1500 years later, the city of Pompeii was discovered, preserved almost perfectly by the lava. Today you can see houses, gardens and even people turned into stone.

- **Off the coast of the Micronesian island** Pohnpei, is the lost city of Nan Madol. It covers 11 square miles of an ancient coral reef and has hundreds of man-made canals and submerged tunnels. It might date from 200BC.

- **In 1845**, the palace of the Assyrian Emperor Sennacherib was discovered in Nineveh – now part of Mosul, Iraq's second largest city.

- **The capital city of the Inca empire**, Machu Picchu, was buried in the Peruvian jungle for centuries until Hiram Bingham stumbled across it in 1911.

▲ *Some scientists think that Vesuvius erupted in pyroclastic flow in* AD79. *Pyroclastic flow is a volcanic avalanche of hot ash, rock fragments and scorching gas which travels at 160 to 240 kilometres an hour.*

- **No one knows if or where King Arthur's city** and castle of Camelot existed. The site was first mentioned by Chretien de Troyes in the twelfth century.

139

Mothers and matriarchies

- **Most mythologies** we know of come from male-ruled societies – patriarchies. However, earlier cultures (usually farming tribes) lived in female-ruled societies – matriarchies.

▲ *According to a Greek poet called Hesiod, the goddess Aphrodite was born from foam on the sea. One legend says that waves carried her to shore at Paphos in Cyprus.*

- **Matriarchies** grew from the importance of Mother Earth in producing food and of human mothers in producing children.

- **In many matriarchies**, an honoured young man became the queen's sacred king for a year. At the end of this time, he was sacrificed to their great goddess for a plentiful harvest.

- **A great goddess in Ancient Greece** was known by different names including: Gaea, Athena, Hera, Artemis and Aphrodite. When male-dominated myths about Zeus took over, these became less important goddesses.

- **The Aztecs** had a terrifying Mother Earth goddess called Coatlicue who could only be satisfied by human sacrifice.

- **Tlacolteutl was the Aztec goddess of childbirth**, and the mother of the god of maize, Cinteotl, and the goddess of flowers, Xochiquetzal.

- **Celtic mothers-to-be** used to pray for help in childbirth to the goddess Frigga, Odin's wife.

- **In Greek myth**, the hero Oedipus grew up without knowing his parents. A prophecy said that he would one day unknowingly marry his own mother – it came true!

- **Many Christian stories** tell how the mother of Jesus, Our Lady, has appeared through history in visions to young people, such as to Saint Bernadette at Lourdes.

- **The Hopi**, Hokohan and Zuni Native American tribes lived in a matriarchal society. However, their religious ceremonies were mostly held by men, wearing masks to represent nature spirits.

◄ *In the Hopi tribe of Native Americans, women governed their villages and owned all the property, such as the houses.*

141

Trees of life

- **According to Norse myth**, the universe is nine worlds held together in a tree called Yggdrasil.

- **The chief Norse god**, Odin, gained powerful magic by hanging on Yggdrasil for nine days.

- **Early Persians** believed in a tree which grew fruit of immortality, which gave the gods life and strength.

- **The Maya** believed that the universe was laid out in a cross shape, at the centre of which was a life-giving tree.

- **In Mesopotamian myth**, the symbol for the mother goddess Ishtar was a tree of life which looked like a date palm.

- **In Chinese mythology**, the ruler of the eastern sky and his children – ten suns – lived in a palace built in an enormous mulberry tree.

- **Ancient Indians** pressed a mountain plant to produce a sacred liquid, called Soma. This was offered to the gods as a sacrifice.

- **According to the Bacongo people of Zaire**, the god Nzambi created the first intelligent life in the form of a palm tree. This eventually separated into a woman and a man.

- **In Syrian mythology**, Fatima is goddess of the Moon and fate. She is pictured as the Tree of Paradise.

- **The Irish Celts** had a calendar which cited a sacred tree for every month of the year.

▶ *According to Norse legend, evil creatures continually tried to destroy the world tree, Yggdrasil, by chewing on its roots, trunk, branches and leaves. A squirrel called Ratatosk scampered up and down every day, carrying messages from top to bottom.*

Fertility mythology

- **Farmer's wives in Ancient Greece** often set an extra place at the table hoping that the goddess of the harvest, Demeter, would bless them by joining them at their meal.

- **Each April**, the Aztecs smeared reeds with their blood and offered them to Cinteotl, the god of maize, to ensure a good food supply.

- **The Japanese goddess of fertility and nourishment** for all life was called Uke-Mochi-No-Kami.

- **An Iroquois Native American myth tells** how the corn goddess, Onatah, was kidnapped by the ruler of the Underworld. During the time her mother searched for her, no crops grew. This tale is similar to a Greek myth about the goddess Demeter and her daughter Persephone.

▲ *According to myth, the cornucopia was the horn of a goat whose milk had fed the god Zeus. It is shown in art overflowing with fruit and vegetables and all the goodness of the harvest.*

- **In Egyptian mythology**, the fertility goddess Hathor was represented as a cow.

- **According to Slavic legend**, Simargl was a creature like a winged dog. He was responsible for scattering the seeds of every plant across the world.

- **In Sumerian mythology**, Tammuz was god of agriculture. He died each year and was brought back from the Underworld by his lover, Ishtar.

- **The Incas** often sacrificed llamas to a fertility goddess called Pachamama.

- **In Ancient Indian mythology**, the god Indra fights a dragon of drought and releases seven rivers which make the Earth fertile again.

- **Baal** was an important fertility god widely worshipped by ancient peoples in the Middle East.

▲ *The Inca used to sacrifice llamas to their fertility goddess. Modern-day Peruvians use llamas as pack-animals and also weave their wool into bright, warm textiles.*

145

Babies and children

- **The Ashanti of Africa** say that a snake taught the first man and woman how to have babies.

- **The Pygmies of Africa** believe that humans were told how to have children by the Moon.

- **The Chaga people of Africa** have a myth in which a mountain spirit turns four gourds into children as company for a sad, lonely widow woman.

- **In Celtic legend**, the Little People or faeries sometimes swap a human baby for a faery one. The faery baby is called a changeling.

- **The Greeks** worshipped Hera as goddess of marriage and childbirth. Her Roman name, Juno, is why it is traditionally lucky to get married in June.

- **Newly married couples in China** pray to a kind goddess called Kwan Yin for help in conceiving a baby.

- **Lupercalia was a Roman festival** in which shepherds made goatskin whips and ran through the streets striking anyone they met. Women believed this would make them more likely to bear children!

▲ *A gourd is from a family of marrow-like vegetables called squashes. The flesh can be eaten and the skin dried to make bottles and bowls and cups.*

▲ *The modern-day myth of Santa Claus developed from the story of Saint Nicholas.*

- **Greek myth** says that when the hero Heracles was a baby, the goddess Hera sent two huge snakes to kill him. Heracles simply strangled them!

- **In Japanese mythology**, Kishi-Bojin is a goddess who protects children.

- **Traditionally, European countries** celebrated the feast of Saint Nicholas on 6 December by giving presents to children. This gradually developed into the myth of Santa Claus.

147

Tales of beauty

◀ *This life-sized statue of the goddess Venus (Greek name: Aphrodite) is around 2100 years old. She is called the Venus de Milo, because she was found on the island of Milos in the Aegean Sea during the second century BC. Today you can see her in the Louvre art gallery and museum in Paris, France.*

● **In Greek myth**, the goddesses Hera, Athena and Aphrodite wanted to know who was the most beautiful. The chief god, Zeus, asked a Trojan prince called Paris to decide. Paris picked Aphrodite, because she promised him the most beautiful woman in the world.

● **Classical myth says that the most** beautiful woman in the world was Helen, queen of Sparta – the daughter of Zeus and the goddess Nemesis.

● **Paris seized Helen** as his reward and stole her away to Troy. This action caused the start of the Trojan Wars.

● **According to Greek myth**, Aphrodite was goddess of beauty and love. At her birth, she emerged from the sea naked and fully grown, and the winds blew her ashore.

● **The Romans adopted Aphrodite under the name of Venus**. Venus was also the official protector of the Roman people.

● **In Hindu myth**, Lakshmi was the goddess of beauty and good fortune.

148

- **The Norse goddess of beauty**, Freya, drove a chariot pulled by two large cats.

- **The Celts** had a god of beauty and love – Angus Og.

- **A Celtic story** says that the wizard Math magicked a beautiful wife for the hero Llew Llaw Gyffes out of blossoms. She was named Blodeuwedd, or 'flower face'.

- **The legend of Beauty and the Beast** was first recorded by a French writer called Madame Gabrielle de Villeneuve, in 1740. In 1756, Madame Le Prince de Beaumont rewrote it into the version most people know today.

▲ *Legend says that the kidnapping of Helen, queen of Sparta, by Prince Paris of Troy caused the start of the Trojan Wars. However, one version of the ancient story says that Helen ran away with Paris willingly.*

Stories of strength

- **The Greek hero Heracles** had superhuman strength from birth.

- **According to Norse myth**, the god Thor once found he was not strong enough to pick up the giant king's cat. It turned out to be the enormous world serpent, Jormungand, disguised by magic.

- **In Japanese legend**, Kintaro ('the golden boy') had amazing strength. In one story, he uprooted a tree and smashed a giant spider over the head with it.

- **Hindus believe that the god Shiva** is the special strengthener of warriors.

- **In Persian myth**, the strength of Mother Earth was given the form of a bull, which roamed the Earth for 3000 years. The god Mithras finally killed it, and its strength went to the gods in the heavens.

- **According to Greek myth**, the Titan Atlas holds the sky on his shoulders.

- **Norse stories say that the gods tethered a monster** named Fenris Wolf with a ribbon called Gleipnir. It looked flimsy, but was made of dwarf-magic and was stronger than any chain.

▲ *The Bible story of Samson and Delilah is told in the Book of Judges, Chapters 13 to 16.*

- **The ancient Japanese sport** of Sumo is a type of wrestling performed by huge strongmen. According to legend, the first Sumo match took place between the Japanese god Take-mikazuchi and the leader of a rival race, to decide who should live in the Japanese islands.

- **The Bible tells of an Israelite hero called Samson** who had superhuman strength – as long as he never had his hair cut.

- **Today, a modern myth about a warrior princess** called Xena has been created for a TV series. Xena not only has amazing strength, she also knows powerful magic.

◀ The sport of Sumo wrestling began in Japan around 20BC The heaviest Sumo wrestlers weigh 250 kg, which is twice as heavy as the heaviest world-champion boxer.

Old age and long life

- **In Classical myth**, a prophetess called the Sibyl wished to live for 1000 years. However, she forgot to ask for eternal youth. She gradually aged and shrunk until she had to live in a bottle.

- **In another Classical myth**, the goddess Eos asked Zeus to make her lover Tithonus immortal. She too forgot to ask for eternal youth, and Tithonus became a withered old man for ever.

- **The modern film** *Highlander* created a myth about a race of warriors who only die if their heads are cut off. Many of the warriors live for centuries!

- **The American writer Washington Irving** (1783–1832) wrote a story called *Rip Van Winkle* based on a Dutch legend. Rip nods off in a dwarf cavern and wakes to find that he is 20 years older!

- **A Norse story** tells how a wrinkled old woman called Elli once wrestled the great god Thor to one knee. Elli was Old Age in disguise – and Old Age defeats everyone in the end.

- **The Chinese god, Shou Lao**, decides how long a person will live. He is often pictured with a turtle or a white crane – symbols of long life.

- **In Japanese mythology**, tortoises and storks often symbolize old age.

▲ *The story* Rip Van Winkle *was first published in 1820, in a collection of tales called* The Sketch Book of Geoffrey Crayon.

- **In Celtic legend**, the goddess Niamh carried away an Irish prince called Oisin to the Land of Youth, Tir Nan Og. When Oisin returned home, he had been away for 300 years!

- **In Celtic myth**, Lir was the Old Man of the Sea. His second wife secretly turned his children into swans and drove them away. By the time Lir found them and reversed the spell, they had become old people themselves.

- **According to the Bible**, in the early days of the world, people lived much longer than they do now. Noah lived for 950 years!

▲ *The white crane is the sacred bird of Japan. Legend says that it lives for 1000 years and that anyone who folds 1000 paper cranes will also live a long life.*

Legendary partnerships

- **Robert Leroy Parker and Harry Longabaugh** were American outlaws who held up banks and trains in the 1890s. They became known in legend as Butch Cassidy and the Sundance Kid.

- **The Norse gods** Thor and Loki once partnered up to win back Thor's magic hammer from a giant who had stolen it. They went to the giant's castle disguised as a bride and bridesmaid!

- **The American legend** of lovers Bonnie Parker and Clyde Barrow tells how they went on a spree of robbery and murder before being shot dead by police in 1934.

- **In Greek myth**, Scylla was a monster who lived in a clifftop cave above a whirlpool called Charybis. Passing ships had to travel between them.

▲ *Legend says that the outlaw Robin Hood and his band of Merry Men lived in Sherwood Forest, near Nottingham in England.*

- **In Afro-Caribbean animal legends** written by Uncle Remus, the wily Brer Rabbit always outsmarts his arch-enemy, Brer Fox.

- **A Wild West legend** says that the outlaw Billy the Kid was close friends with a sheriff called Pat Garrett. Some believe that Garrett helped the Kid fake his own death to escape the law.

- **English legends about a hero** called Robin Hood who teamed up with a gang of Merry Men to rob the rich and give to the poor have been told since the fourteenth century.

▲ *Adam West played Batman and Burt Ward played Robin in a TV series about the superhero partners filmed from 1966 to 1968.*

- **The legendary superhero Batman** first appeared as a cartoon in detective comics in 1937. His sidekick, Robin, did not appear until 1940.

- **According to the Fon people of Africa**, the world remains fertile due to the partnership of Sagbata, god of the earth, and Sogbo, god of the sky. Sagbata gives Sogbo control of the earth and all living things, as long as Sogbo sends down life-giving rain.

- **Modern ballet dancers** strive to achieve the standard of Margot Fonteyn and Rudolph Nureyev, who became a legendary partnership in the 1960s.

Learning and knowledge

- **According to Norse myth**, the chief warrior god, Odin, bought a drink from the Fountain of Knowledge at the foot of the World Tree. The price was one of his own eyes.

- **Ancient Egyptians believed that it was their god of wisdom**, Thoth, who had devised laws, worked out how to measure time, and invented hieroglyphic writing.

- **The Celtic goddess of learning was called Brigid**. This means 'the powerful one'.

▲ *The Ancient Egyptians used hieroglyphics to write inscriptions on the walls of tombs and temples, and to write religious texts on papyrus scrolls. Only priests and scribes knew how to write.*

- **According to Inca legend,** the creator god Viraccocha roamed the world to teach mankind wisdom. However, people were too busy with crime and war to listen.

- **In Chinese myth,** Guan Di is the wise god of law, martial arts and diplomacy.

- **Japanese people** believed that it was their god of learning, Tenjin, who taught them how to write.

- **In Tibetan** Buddhism, eight giant warriors called Dharmapalas have the power to scorch enemies of Truth with the light of perfect knowledge.

- **The Hindu god of learning is Hanuman,** who is half-human, half-monkey.

- **According to Muslim Shia stories,** teachers called Sayyids are direct descendants of the Prophet Muhammad who are gifted with learning from birth.

> ····FASCINATING FACT····
> The Maori people of New Zealand traditionally recite their culture of myth in a long chant called Wharewananga. This means 'school of learning'.

Tragic love stories

- **In Greek myth**, Narcissus was a handsome youth who fell in love with his own reflection. He killed himself in despair.

- **Possibly the most famous legendary lovers** are the Roman General, Mark Antony, an the 'enemy' queen of Egypt, Cleopatra, who lived around 40BC Due to the conflict in Antony's loyalties, he committed suicide.

- **According to Aztec myth**, the god of the wind, Ehecatl, fell in love with a mortal calle Mayahuel. Unfortunately, his divine lovemaking killed her!

- **The famous ballet** *Giselle* is based on a German legend abo a girl who dies of a broken hea

- **Classical myth says that** Dido, queen of Carthage, killed herself when her Trojan lover, Aeneas, was told by the gods to leave h

- **A South American myth** says that a woman called Cavillaca fled from the passionate advances the creator god Coniray They were both turned into rocks in the sea.

▲ *When Queen Cleopatra of Egypt discovered that Antony had committed suicide, she killed herself too. On their deaths, in 30BC, Egypt was taken by the Roman Empire.*

- **The tragic love story of Romeo and Juliet** was not Shakespeare's idea. The tale existed in different forms for thousands of years before the great playwright magically reworked it.

- **One of the earliest** Romeo and Juliet stories was Babylonian. A youth called Pyramus was led to believe that his lover, Thisbe, was dead. He killed himself– but Thisbe was in fact alive and well! In grief, she committed suicide.

▲ *The love affair between King Arthur's wife, Guinevere, and his best friend, Sir Lancelot, first entered Arthurian legend in the stories of the French writer Chretien de Troyes in the twelfth century.*

- **The love affair between King Arthur's wife**, Guinevere, and his best friend, Sir Lancelot, brought no one happiness. Lancelot was banished and the alliance of the Knights of the Round Table collapsed. The weakened Arthur was killed and the remorseful Guinevere went to live in a convent.

- **Arthurian legend** says that Merlin fell in love with the Lady of the Lake and taught her all the secrets of his sorcery. She repaid the magician by imprisoning him in a glass tower.

Living happily ever after

- **In Greek myth**, Penelope was the wife of the hero Ulysses. She waited faithfully for 20 years for her husband to return from the Trojan Wars.

- **The Japanese goddess of love, Benten**, once set out to get rid of an evil Serpent King. However, the couple fell in love! Benten made the Serpent King promise to change his ways and they were happily married.

- **According to one Robin Hood myth**, the folk hero rescued Maid Marian from the advances of King John I and married her himself.

- **A Chinese myth** tells how a servant once disguised himself as a magical rainbow-coloured dog and won the emperor's permission to marry his daughter.

▲ *The Queen of Faery has terrifying magical powers in the Scottish legend of Tam Lin.*

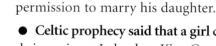

- **Celtic prophecy said that a girl called Deirdre** would bring ruin on Ireland, so King Conchobar of Ulster hid her away in a castle deep in a forest. She managed to escape to Scotland with the king's own nephew.

- **The Greek hero Perseus** rescued Andromeda from being sacrificed to a sea monster. Their names live on as constellations of stars.

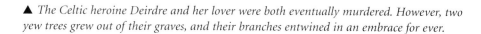

▲ *The Celtic heroine Deirdre and her lover were both eventually murdered. However, two yew trees grew out of their graves, and their branches entwined in an embrace for ever.*

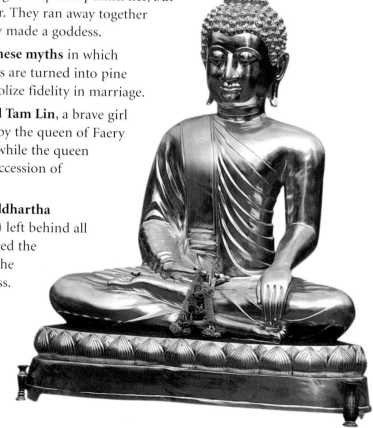

- **According to Roman myth**, Psyche was a girl who boasted that she was more beautiful than the goddess Venus. Venus sent the god Cupid to punish her, but he fell in love with her. They ran away together and Psyche was finally made a goddess.

- **There are many Japanese myths** in which devoted, faithful lovers are turned into pine trees. Pine trees symbolize fidelity in marriage.

- **In the Scottish legend Tam Lin**, a brave girl wins a man captured by the queen of Faery by holding him tight while the queen changes him into a succession of terrifying creatures.

- **The Indian prince Siddhartha Gautama** (563–483BC) left behind all his riches, and wandered the world until he found the secret of true happiness. He became known as the Buddha.

▶ *The Buddha taught that people should aim to achieve absolute peace – a state called nirvana.*

161

Tales of inspiration and courage

▲ *Mahatma Ghandi's real name was Mohandas Ghandi. His followers called him 'the Mahatma' which means 'great soul'.*

● **On 29 September 1914** a story by William Machen appeared in the *London Evening News* about angels helping British soldiers in a World War I battle at Mons in France. Machen later realized he had created a modern myth when he came across other versions of his story, all claiming to be true.

● **The legend of Joan of Arc** tells how a young peasant girl led the armies of the king of France in the fifteenth century. She was burnt as a witch, but centuries later made a saint.

● **A Swiss legend says that a man called William Tell** was once forced to shoot an arrow at an apple balanced on his son's head – which the hero did safely.

● **Hindus tell legends of Mahatma Ghandi** (1869–1948). He was a Hindu leader who led peaceful protests against British rule in India and in support of rights for the poorest Indians.

● **In 1838, lighthouse keeper's daughter Grace Darling** bravely rowed through stormy seas to rescue nine survivors of a shipwreck on the Farne Islands. She became a Victorian legend.

● **Classical legend tells how around 2200 years ago**, a brilliant Carthaginian general called Hannibal used elephants to cross the Alps to battle the Romans in the Second Punic War.

- **The legend of Spartacus** tells the story of an escaped Roman gladiator who from 73–71BC led 120,000 runaway slaves in an uprising for their freedom.

- **In 1297**, William Wallace led a Scottish uprising against the English. Legends tell of the hero's passion for national freedom.

- **The nun Mother Teresa** spent 50 years nursing the sick and dying among the poorest people in Calcutta. Since her death in 1997, stories have spread telling that sick people are now being miraculously healed in her name.

- **The legend of nurse Florence Nightingale** (1820–1910) suggests she was an angelic 'lady with a lamp'. In fact, this pioneering woman was tough, driven and highly organized.

▼ *Sir William Wallace raised and led a force of Scottish freedom-fighters against the might of the English army. He is one of Scotland's greatest national heroes and was immortalized in the 1995 Hollywood movie,* Braveheart.

Stories of fire

- **Stories say that the Greek god Zeus** did not want humans to have the secret of fire. A Titan called Prometheus stole fire and gave it to humans.

- **The Kayapo tribes of South America** believe that a jaguar once adopted an abandoned boy called Botoque and taught him the secret of how to make fire.

- **In Ancient Persian myth**, Atar was the god of fire and defender of creation.

- **In the Persian religion of Zoroastrianism**, fire is the symbol of the creator god, Ahura Mazda. Zoroastrians worship in fire temples.

- **A circular temple to Vesta**, goddess of fire, stood in the heart of Rome in the Forum. A sacred flame was kept always burning there.

- **The ancient Hindu fire god Agni** was worshipped for his warmth and light, but also feared for his powers of destruction.

- **According to Lithuanian myth**, Kalvaitis was a blacksmith god who remade the sun each day and sent it red-hot across the sky.

- **Hephaestus was blacksmith to the Greek gods**. His fiery furnace was believed to lie under the volcano Mount Etna in Sicily. The Roman name for Hephaestus was Vulcan.

- **In a South Pacific myth**, the god Maui tricked the goddess Mahui-Ike into giving him the gift of fire. When she realized, she was so furious that she set the whole world ablaze.

- **In Japanese mythology**, when the spirit of fire, Kagutsuchi, was born, he scorched his mother so badly that she died.

▶ *According to Hindu belief, the fire god Agni acts as a link between people and the heavens, because the smoke from his sacred flames rises up into the skies. He is shown with three heads, above which flames flicker, riding on a ram called Vahana.*

Friendships with animals

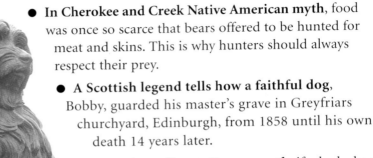

- **In Cherokee and Creek Native American myth,** food was once so scarce that bears offered to be hunted for meat and skins. This is why hunters should always respect their prey.

- **A Scottish legend tells how a faithful dog,** Bobby, guarded his master's grave in Greyfriars churchyard, Edinburgh, from 1858 until his own death 14 years later.

- **According to Roman myth,** if a hedgehog peeped out of its burrow on 2 February and saw a shadow, there would be six more weeks of winter. The American ritual of Groundhog Day is based on a similar belief.

- **A story recorded by a Greek slave called Aesop** tells how a man called Androcles was thrown to a lion in an amphitheatre. However, the lion refused to eat him. Androcles had once pulled a thorn from its injured paw!

- **In 1912,** Edgar Rice Burroughs wrote a book about a child who was brought up by gorillas in the jungle. The legend of Tarzan was born.

▲ *A statue in Greyfriars churchyard, Edinburgh, commemorates the remarkable faithfulness of a dog called Bobby.*

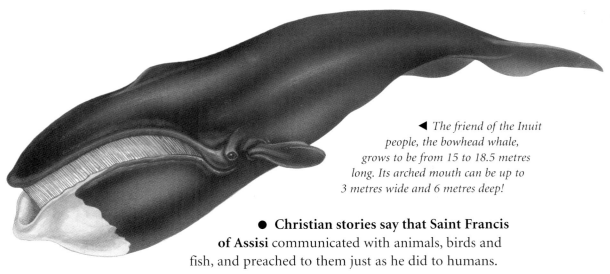

◄ *The friend of the Inuit people, the bowhead whale, grows to be from 15 to 18.5 metres long. Its arched mouth can be up to 3 metres wide and 6 metres deep!*

● **Christian stories say that Saint Francis of Assisi** communicated with animals, birds and fish, and preached to them just as he did to humans.

● **The legendary hero** the Lone Ranger rode a faithful white horse whom he summoned with the shout, 'Hi-yo, Silver!'

● **A Russian myth** tells how a wise grey wolf helps a Tsar's son called Ivan to search for the legendary firebird.

● **An Inuit myth says that the Supreme Spirit** made the bowhead whale to be their best friend. He allowed the Inuit to hunt the creature for food, skins and tools to survive.

● **In 1956 in Kenya**, a conservationist called Joy Adamson adopted an abandoned lion cub, Elsa, and trained her to return to the wild. Legend says that Joy was eventually mauled to death by a lion. In fact, she was murdered by an ex-employee.

167

Eternal life

- **Egyptian gods** are sometimes pictured holding a symbol called an Ankh as though it were a key. This symbolized the opening of the gates of death to immortality.

- **The Ancient Chinese religion**, Taoism, teaches belief in eight immortals who discovered a magical elixir of life which allowed them to live for ever.

- **In Medieval Europe**, early scientists called alchemists strove to create an elixir of life which would cure all illnesses.

- **The Celtic god Govannon** is a blacksmith who also brews a mead of eternal life.

- **The mischievous Chinese spirit, Monkey**, was once appointed Guardian of the Garden of Immortal Peaches – but he ate all the heavenly fruit and became immortal himself!

- **In Arabic, 'khuld' means eternal life**. Islamic stories teach that all souls are immortal – some will go to heaven and others will go to hell.

- **In Roman mythology**, Jupiter punished a traitor called Janus by giving him immortality but taking away his freedom to move. Janus was made to stand for ever as Heaven's gatekeeper.

▲ *The symbol at the centre of this Taoist shrine is Yin Yang. It represents the balance of calm, female forces in life (Yin) with active, male forces (Yang).*

▲ *The sacred Mount Fuji is the highest mountain in Japan. In summer, people climb to the Shinto shrine at its summit.*

- **Sengen is the Japanese goddess of blossom** and the sacred mountain Fujiyama. She guards the secret Well of Eternal Youth.
- **In Chinese myth**, cranes are used as symbols of immortality.
- **In Greek myth**, ambrosia was the food of the gods. Anyone who ate it became immortal.

169

Health and healing

- **The Navajo tribe of Native Americans** made coloured sand pictures of spirits, which they believed had the power to heal.

- **Iroquois Native American myth** tells how a tribe was once dying of illness. The animals prayed to the Supreme Spirit, who showed a brave called Nekumonta a spring of healing waters.

- **Hindu myth tells of a famous doctor** called Yama-Kumar. His father, the Lord of Death, told him whether or not he would be able to heal each of his patients.

- **Medieval myths** said that the Mandrake plant had healing powers, but that when it was pulled out of the ground, it gave a scream which drove people mad.

- **Legend says that the Brazilian Jose Arigo** (1918–1971) had miraculous psychic powers which enabled him to perform thousands of operations such as eye surgery without any medical training or anaesthetic.

▲ *According to Greek myth, a centaur was a creature with the body and legs of a horse, but the chest, arms and head of a man.*

- **According to Greek myth,** when the sea goddess Thetis had a baby boy by a mortal, she tried to save the child from harm by dipping him in the river Styx. The sacred waters protected the baby everywhere except the one heel she was holding. The child grew up to be the hero Achilles.

- **Asclepius, the Greek god of healing**, was taught the arts of medicine and surgery by a wise centaur called Chiron.

- **In Ancient Persian** myth, the hero Thrita could protect humans from disease and death because his prayers brought forth plants of healing.

- **The Inuit god of healing** was Eeyeekalduk. He was depicted as a tiny old man who lived inside a pebble.

- **The Japanese god of medicine**, Sukuna-Biko, was so small that he could rest on a stalk of millet.

▶ *Mandrake root is famous for being a chief ingredient in witches' brews. According to legend, it was only safe to pull the plant out of the ground after performing a special chant and ritual in the moonlight.*

Struggle with fate

- **According to gypsy belief,** there are three female spirits of fate. Two are good, but one seeks to harm humans.

- **Norse myth tells of three women** who decide the fate of humans – the Norns.

- **The Greeks and Romans** also believed in three women who set destiny, called the Fates.

- **The Vikings** believed that even their warrior gods were fated to die one day.

- **Although the Classical gods** and goddesses often helped their favourite mortals, they never tried to change their destined deaths.

▲ *In Classical myth, the Fates were represented as three women spinning thread. Each piece of thread represented a human life. The Fates decided how long or short it should be.*

▼ *Historians think that Delphi was a sacred site in Greece long before the worship of the god Apollo in Ancient times. Female figurines dating back to the twelfth century BC have been found there, which indicates that an early earth goddess was worshipped there.*

- **The Greeks believed that the god Apollo** told what was fated to happen through an oracle at Delphi in Greece.

- **Today in Italy**, you can still see the cave at Cumae where a famous seer called the Sibyl spoke of things fated to happen.

- **The Fon god of fate, Legba,** is shown as an old man leaning on a stick, which he uses to prop up the universe.

- **Slavic peoples believed that the spirits of female ancestors** appeared at the cradle of a newborn baby and decided its destiny.

- **The Celts did not fear fate**, as they believed that death was merely a passage from this life to a happy land where everyone lived in eternal bliss.

Warnings and curses

- **Celtic peoples** believed that anyone who heard the wail of a spirit woman called a Banshee would soon die.

- **In Greek myth**, the inventor Daedalus made wings for himself and his son Icarus, to escape from prison. Daedalus warned Icarus not to fly too near to the sun, but Icarus forgot. His wings burned and he plunged to his death in the ocean.

▲ *The word 'banshee' comes from the Irish Gaelic 'bean sidhe', which literally means 'woman of the fairy mound'.*

- **According to the Eastern Orthodox Church**, the body of anyone bound by a curse will not decay, so they cannot find peace.

- **In 1798**, Coleridge wrote a poem called *The Rime of the Ancient Mariner* based on an ancient curse: any sailor who shoots a huge seabird called an albatross brings doom upon his crew.

- **Medieval legends say that the 'Wandering Jew'** was a man who mocked Jesus when he was carrying his cross. Jesus cursed him to walk the Earth till the end of time.

- **In English myth**, a Grant looks like a bright prancing horse. Anyone who sees it is cursed with bad luck.

- **The Greek god Zeus** cursed a prophet called Phineas for being too truthful to mortals. Whenever Phineas sat down to eat, creatures called Harpies swooped down and snatched his food away.

- **In 387BC**, a Roman called Caedicius heard a voice for several days warning that the city walls should be strengthened. The Roman authorities did not believe him. Not long afterwards, invading armies of Gauls arrived and found the city almost undefended.

- **According to German myth**, if you see your own double (or 'doppelganger') it is a warning that you will soon die.

- **Christians believe that** the Curse of Eve is the pain women suffer during childbirth.

▶ The Rime of the Ancient Mariner *warned that any sailor that shot an albatross brought doom upon his crew.*

175

Wrath and punishment

- **Egyptian myth** says that illnesses were brought into the world by the lion-headed goddess Sekhmet to punish humans, who were turning against the sun god, Ra-Atum.

- **A Greek nymph called Echo** once so annoyed Zeus by being a chatterbox that he took away her speech. From then on, she could only repeat the words of others.

- **German legend says that in 1284** a mysterious musician called the Pied Piper rid the town of Hamelin of a plague of rats. When the townspeople refused to pay him, the Pied Piper lured their children away as a punishment.

- **In Greek myth**, an evil king called Tantalus was punished in the Underworld by being chained up near to water and food. Every time he reached for it, it moved away.

- **Hittite myth** says that the world is punished when the bad-tempered fertility god Telepinu is angry, as nothing will then grow.

▶ *The nineteenth-century poet, Robert Browning, turned the legend of the Pied Piper of Hamelin into an extremely popular children's poem.*

▶ *This Viking carving shows the Norse trickster Loki. Half-god and half-giant, he was often friendly, fun company for the gods, but ultimately turned malicious.*

- **In 1909**, 19-year-old Robert Stroud began a lifetime in various American prisons for manslaughter and other violent crimes. He spent years studying birds and became known in legend as the Birdman of Alcatraz.

- **The Greeks believed** in a goddess responsible for punishing wrong-doers, called Nemesis.

- **According to Chinese myth**, Buddha punished the naughty Monkey by making him accompany a young priest on a journey from India to bring Buddhist teachings to China.

- **The wicked Norse god Loki** was punished by being bound to a rock in fetters made from his own son's body. A snake was then fixed to drip venom on his head for the rest of time.

- **According to Greek myth**, Zeus punished the Titan Prometheus for giving humans the secret of fire by nailing him to a mountain and setting an eagle to tear out his liver every day.

Flood mythology

- **Historians think that many flood myths**, including the Bible tale of Noah's Ark, may have arisen from a catastrophic flood that occurred between 3000 and 2000BC in Mesopotamia.

- **The Sumerian epic poem *Gilgamesh*** tells how the ruler of the gods, Enlil, sent a flood to destroy the world. A man named Utanapishtim built an ark and saved his family, together with specimens of every animal, bird and plant.

- **Greek myth** tells that Zeus once flooded the world. A man called Deucalion and his wife, Pyrrha, survived by building a boat and filling it with provisions.

- **According to Norse myth**, a flood killed all the Rime Giants except one. The wise Bergelmir survived by building a roofed boat for himself and his family.

- **The Mandan Native Americans** believed that animals once helped a hero build a huge canoe to save their tribe from a terrible flood.

- **A Chinese myth says that the thunder god** once flooded the whole world. The only two humans to survive were a little boy and girl who hollowed out a gourd into a boat.

- **According to Guarani and Caribbean flood myths**, the survivors escaped not by building boats but by climbing tall trees.

- **Inca myth says that the sun god** once flooded the world to destroy it, then sent his son, Manco Capac, and his daughter, Mama Ocllo, to the Earth to teach people civilization and proper worship of the Sun.

- **In Borneo myth**, a woman was the sole surivor of a flood which wiped out humans. She mated with the flames of her camp fire and repopulated the world.

- **According to the Tupinamba of South America**, Monan the creator grew fed up with ungrateful humans and destroyed the world by fire. He saved one man, Irin-Mage, who begged Monan to quench the fire with a huge flood and give the world a second chance.

▼ *The Bible story of the Flood can be found in the Book of Genesis. It says that Noah's Ark came to rest at the top of Mount Ararat, which is in modern-day Turkey.*

How evil and death entered the world

- **Many African tribes believe** that death entered the world by mistake. For instance, Burundi myth says that the creator was chasing death out of the world when a woman got in his way, so death escaped to freedom.

- **In Banyarwanda myth**, the creator once hunted Death. He told everything to stay indoors, so Death could not hide. But an old woman went out to hoe her vegetable garden, and Death hid under her skirt and was taken inside.

▲ *The myth of Pandora's Box says that evils and sorrows flew into the world like stinging insects. However, the Box also contained a bright-winged butterfly – hope.*

- **According to Greek myth**, a girl called Pandora opened a forbidden sealed box. It contained every evil and sorrow, and they all flew out into the world.

- **According to some Native American myths**, the god Coyote decided that humans should die. He regretted this bitterly when he could not save his own son from a snake bite.

◀ *The Voodoo god of death, Ghede, is also known as King Cholera.*

180

- **A Caraja myth from South America** says that the first humans lived underground and were immortal. When they discovered the beautiful land above the Earth, many people stayed and lived there, even though they would one day become old and die.

- **According to Norse myth**, a giantess witch called Gullveig once wandered about the world of humans, bringing sin and misery.

- **The Navajo Native Americans** believed that all evils entered the world from the east: sickness, wars and white people.

- **A myth from New Zealand says** that the Dawn-maiden once unknowingly committed a crime and fled to the Underworld. Ever since, she has dragged people down to the land of the dead to be with her.

- **A Sudanese myth** tells how the mother of a dead child once begged the god Ajok to bring her baby back to life. When the father found out he was horrified, and killed the child again. From then on, Ajok left death as permanent among his people.

▲ *In the mythologies of many European countries, Death is pictured as being a silent figure in a dark cloak. His hood hides his face – a skull. He sometimes carries a scythe with which he cuts short human lives, and is then called 'the Grim Reaper'.*

- **In Papua New Guinean myth**, Honoyeta was a demon who could take on the form of a human or a snake. One day, one of his wives burnt his snakeskin, so he was stuck in his human form for ever. As retaliation, Honoyeta brought death to humans.

Legendary 'baddies'

- **The Roman Emperor Caligula** was an evil tyrant who hated his own people and delighted in torture. He was born in AD12 and murdered in AD41.

- **Ghengis Khan was a ruthless military leader** who united the Mongol tribes into an empire around AD1200. He destroyed anyone or anything that stood in his way.

- **The most famous American gangster,** Al Capone, was born in Brooklyn, New York in 1899. He lived a life of crime in Chicago and died in 1947 – not through mob warfare, but from ill health.

- **Edward Teach is better known as the pirate, Blackbeard.** His career on the high seas only lasted two years before he was killed in 1718, but during that time he attacked so many ships that he became the most famous pirate ever.

- **Anne Bonny and Mary Read** were two women pirates caught on a ship called the *Revenge* in 1720. They were sentenced to be hanged, but Anne mysteriously disappeared from prison, and Mary died of fever.

- **Attila was a savage warrior** who united the Hun tribes of Eastern Europe into a mighty empire in the fifth century. The Romans called him 'the Scourge of God', because of the destruction he wreaked on their realms.

- **A story says that in Victorian times** a penniless barber called Sweeny Todd lived in Fleet Street in London. He killed his customers and stole their money, and a woman neighbour made the bodies into tasty pies!

- **Ghede (or Baron Samedi)** is the sinister god of the dead in Haitian Voodoo mythology. He wears dark glasses and a black tail-coat and top hat, and loves to drink rum!

- **European myth** tells of a man called Faustus who sold his soul to the devil in return for earthly power and riches.

● **According to some Jewish and Islamic stories,** the first woman God created was not Eve, but Lilith. However, Lilith ran away from Adam and slept with Satan, bearing demon children.

▲ *Legend says that before battle, Blackbeard braided his famous bushy whiskers into pigtails. Then he stuck slow burning matches into them so his face was wreathed in smoke – reminiscent of a terrifying demon from hell.*

Burial beliefs

▶ *Vultures and birds called condors feed mainly on dead and dying animals, known as carrion.*

- **The Greeks believed that Hades**, god of the Underworld, taught burial practices to mortals, to show respect for the dead.

- **The Bushpeople of Botswana** believe that Gauna (or Death) taught them burial rituals in order to keep ghosts in their graves.

- **Zoroastrians** believe that dead bodies provide a home for Angra Mainy, the force of evil. They are left out for vultures.

- **In Java**, stories say that anyone who wishes to receive a message from a spirit should spend the night alone in the mortuary.

- **Arthurian legend** says that Lancelot once captured a castle called Dolorous Gard. When he explored it, he found a tomb with his own name on it. It was where he was destined to be buried.

◀ *Tribal peoples in Indonesia traditionally try to impress the gods with the importance of a dead person, so their spirit is allowed into heaven. After a party that goes on for days, the corpse is laid in a burial cave, to become part of a display of hundreds of skulls and skeletons.*

- **In Finnish myth,** the goddess of death and decay, Kalma, is believed to haunt graves, snatching the flesh of the dead.

- **The Greeks and Romans** believed a dead body (or its burnt ashes) should be covered with earth – even a symbolic couple of handfuls was enough. If it was not, the dead person's soul would not find its way into the Underworld.

- **When the Greek hero, Jason,** was fleeing from the king of Colchis, the witchgirl Medea cut up the king's son (her brother) and scattered the pieces of his body behind Jason's ship. The pursuing king stopped to collect the pieces in order to give his son a proper burial, so Jason and his crew of Argonauts escaped.

- **Hindu stories** say that if the ashes of a dead person are scattered on the river Ganges at the holy city of Varanasi, their soul will be nearer to breaking out of an endless circle of death and rebirth, and so closer to attaining heaven.

- **At a Chinese funeral,** mourners burn fake money. This is as an offering to the gods of the Underworld, so they will allow the dead person to pass through and reach heaven.

▼ *In Mexico, 1 November is celebrated as the Day of the Dead, when people believe their dead loved ones will visit them at home. Shops sell skeleton toys, cake coffins and bread bones which people buy to leave as offerings for the spirits.*

185

Underworlds

- **Classical myth** says that a terrifying three-headed dog called Cerberus guarded the entrance to the Underworld.

- **Ancient Greeks believed** that if a god or goddess swore an oath on an underworld river called the Styx, they were not allowed to break it.

  - **The Greeks believed** that another river in the Underworld was called the Lethe. Each spirit drank from it to forget their past life.

◀ *Greek myth tells how the hero Heracles tied up the three-headed hell-hound Cerberus, dragged him to the court of King Eurystheus, then returned him to the Underworld.*

- **According to the Ainu of Japan,** all souls go to an underworld called Pokna-Moshiri where the good are rewarded and the bad are punished.

- **In Welsh mythology,** a cauldron of the Underworld is owned by a goddess called Cerridwen. She uses it to brew a mead of divine knowledge and inspiration.

- **Mictlan** is the ninth and lowest level of the Mayan Underworld. It is the cold, dark realm of the wicked.

- **In the mythology of Finland,** the Underworld is called Tuonela. It is a place of diseases and corpse-eating monsters.

- **The queen of the Norse** Underworld was Hela, the goddess of death. She was half-living, half-corpse. She ruled over the spirits of those who did not die in battle.

- **In Libyan mythology,** the Underworld is ruled by the goddess of death and prophecy, Echidne. She is half-woman, half-serpent.

. . . **FASCINATING FACT** . . .
The Iroquois Native Americans believed that forces called Ohdows controlled the Underworld and stopped spirits coming to the surface.

Pictures of paradise

- **The Celts believed** that various 'otherworlds' existed. Tir Nan Og (or Tir inna Beo) was a paradise which looked like Earth, only far more beautiful.

- **According to Celtic myth**, one peaceful refuge for blessed spirits was the enchanted island of Avalon.

- **One Celtic myth** said that a man called Donn, who was one of their ancestors – the Children of Mil – was buried on a small island off the coast of Ireland. They believed Donn would welcome their spirits to live with him.

- **In some Classical myths**, Elysium is a happy realm at the ends of the earth for heroes. In others, it is a peaceful place in the Underworld where good souls rest before being reborn.

- **According to Norse myth**, warriors who died bravely in battle were taken by female spirits called Valkyries to the gods' home, Asgard. They lived there in a palace called Valhalla.

- **Tillan-Tlapaallan** is one of three Aztec heavens. It is reserved for those who share in the wisdom of the god Quetzalcoatl.

▶ *The Celtic paradise of Tir Nan Og was a beautiful land without illness, old age or death.*

▶ *The Bible tells how the first man and woman lived in a paradise on Earth called the Garden of Eden. When the first woman, Eve, was tempted into eating forbidden fruit, the couple were cast out into the world of sin and suffering.*

- **According to Fijian myth**, Burotu is an island of eternal life and joy where the souls of good people will go to rest in the cool shade.

- **Islamic stories say that paradise** is a beautiful garden, where the souls of the blessed will live in splendid palaces.

- **In European medieval legend**, the Land of Cockaigne was a paradise for idle, greedy people, where the rivers flowed wine and the buildings were made of cake.

- **Chinese Buddhists** believe in a heavenly paradise where souls appear as flowers before an enlightened female spirit called Dha-shi-zhi.

Pharaohs and pyramids

▼ *The Ancient Egyptians believed that the jackal-headed god, Anubis, brought the souls of the dead into an underworld courtroom to be judged good or bad.*

- **The Ancient Egyptians** believed that people could enjoy life after death by preserving the body through mummification, putting food and personal possessions in their tomb and following elaborate funeral rites.

- **Part of mummification** involved removing the internal organs into pots called canopic jars.

- **Each mummy had a mask**, so every spirit could recognize its body.

- **People believed that they would work in the afterlife**, so models of their tools were buried with them. Pharaohs were buried with model servants called ushabtis, to work for them.

- **The Ancient Egyptians** copied their funeral rites from the funeral the god Horus gave to his father, Osiris. These were written in a work called *The Book of the Dead*.

- **One important funeral rite** was called the Opening of the Mouth ceremony.

- **Egyptian myth** says that the dead person's soul, or 'ka' was brought to an underworld Hall of Judgement.

- **First, a jackal-headed god called Anubis** weighed their heart against a feather of truth and justice. If the heart was heavier than the feather, it was devoured by a crocodile-headed god called Ammit.

- **If the heart was lighter than the feather**, the god Horus led the ka to be welcomed into the Underworld by the god Osiris.

- **People used to think** that the pharaohs enlisted slaves to build their pyramid tombs. Today, many historians think the Ancient Egyptians did this willingly, to please the gods and better their chances for life after death.

▼ *Experts are baffled to this day as to how the Ancient Egyptians built their pyramids. Many theories have been tried out, but modern-day historians cannot explain satisfactorily how such vast quantities of stone could have been moved such huge distances and arranged with such incredible accuracy.*

Descent into the realm of the dead

▲ *Orpheus was told he was allowed to rescue his dead wife from the Underworld, as long as he didn't look at her on the journey back up to the world of the living. Tragically, he couldn't resist.*

● **Greek myth says** that a poet called Orpheus once ventured down to the Underworld to try to bring back his wife, Eurydice.

● **According to Chinese myth**, a certain Buddhist monk once searched the Underworld for the soul of his mother. The gods kept him there as its ruler!

● **Greek myth says that when the** god of the dead kidnapped Persephone, the messenger god, Hermes, went into the Underworld to persuade Hades to let her go.

● **In Norse myth**, the messenger god, Hermod, volunteered to go to the Underworld to try to bring the god Baldur back to life.

● **The 'Harrowing of Hell'** is a legend which says that Jesus journeyed into Hell and triumphed over evils there in the three days between his death and resurrection.

● **In the Roman epic** *The Aeneid*, the hero Aeneas travels to the Underworld where the ghost of his father shows him a line of souls waiting to be born as his descendants.

▲ *This picture of the Egyptian sun god, sailing at night through the Underworld in his Boat of Millions of Years, was found in the Tomb of Anhurkhawi.*

- **The Mayan creator god**, Hunahpu, travelled into the Underworld with his brother, Ixbalangue. There they killed two demons, Hun Came and Vucub Caquix.

- **The Greek hero Odysseus** went into the Underworld to ask a dead seer, Tiresias, how he could find his way home from the Trojan Wars.

- **The Ancient Egyptians** believed that every night the sun god sailed through the Underworld, fighting demons and other evils.

- **A Thracian people** believed that the god Zalmoxis lived among humans. He once disappeared into the Underworld for three years, so he could teach people about the immortality of the soul.

193

Vampire mythology

- **Blood-drinking monsters** have featured in myths for thousands of years. Ancient Greeks believed in creatures called lamiae that ate children and drank bloosd. Stories from India from 3500 years ago tell of vampire-like creatures called Rakshasas.

- **Modern ideas about vampires come from** Eastern Europe: they are pale-skinned 'undead' who sleep in their coffins during the day and come out at night to drink blood and turn other people into vampires.

◄ Garlic is traditionally thought to be a weapon against vampires. Legend says it is also a cure for warts!

- **The word 'vampir'** is Slavic in origin.

- **Another word for vampires** is 'nosferatu'.

- **People believe** there are three ways to kill a vampire:
  (1) drive a wooden stake through the vampire's heart,
  (2) expose the vampire to sunlight,
  (3) set the vampire on fire.

- **Myths say you can ward off** vampires with crucifixes, holy water and garlic.

- **The most famous vampire is Count Dracula**, who lived in a castle in Transylvania in Romania. The myth may have come from the real-life blood-thirsty Romanian tyrant, Vlad the Impaler, who was also known by the name Dracula.

◄ According to Christian stories, evil spirits will shrink away from the image of the dying Christ on a crucifix.

- **Around 1560,** a noblewoman called Elizabeth Bathory killed over 600 girls in order to drink their blood. She believed this would keep her youthful.

- **The rare medical condition porphyria** could account for some vampire myths. It causes sensitivity to sunlight and garlic, and makes gums shrink, giving the incisor teeth the appearance of 'fangs'.

- **Vampire myths** have inspired many famous books, films and TV programmes, including: *Dracula* by Bram Stoker, *Interview with a Vampire* by Ann Rice, *Salem's Lot* by Stephen King, *Blade* starring Wesley Snipes and *Buffy the Vampire Slayer.*

▲ *Legend says that vampires can only attack people at night. During the day, they have to keep away from sunlight by hiding inside their coffins.*

Doom, death and disappearance

◄ *Many people thought that a 'mummy's curse' fell on those who opened Tutankhamun's tomb. Lord Caernarvon, the expedition's financial backer, did in fact die just seven weeks afterwards. However, the leading archaeologist, Howard Carter, lived for another 17 years until the age of 65.*

● **Legend says** that a 'deathly' curse was written upon the tomb of the pharaoh Tutankhamun, discovered by Howard Carter in November 1922. In fact, no such curse was discovered.

● **The Bible story of of the prophet Elijah** says that he didn't die at all, but drove up to heaven in a chariot of fire.

● **Bruce Lee** was a martial artist and film star, who suddenly fell into a coma in July 1973 and died at the age of 32. According to one myth, he was killed by an enemy in the martial arts world who gave him a mysterious 'death touch'.

● **The Russian tsar Nicholas II** and his family were executed on 16 July 1918, after the Russian Revolution. Legend says that one daughter, Anastasia, escaped – but this has never been proved.

● **The legend of Lord Lucan** tells how he vanished, never to be seen again, on 7 November 1974 – the same day that his children's nanny was found murdered at their home.

● **The beautiful Egyptian queen Nefertiti** was the wife of a rebel pharaoh, Akhenaten, who tried to change traditional religious beliefs and made many enemies. No one knows how she died, and her mummy has never been found.

- **Many legends** have arisen around the sinking of the enormous passenger ship RMS *Titanic* on 14 April 1912, when she hit an iceberg on her maiden voyage. A story told by Catholics in Northern Ireland, where the ship was made, said that the *Titanic* was cursed because the shipbuilders gave her the number 3909 04, which looks like 'no pope' if you read it backwards in a mirror.

- **In 1912,** the explorer Laurence Oates became very ill on an Antarctic expedition led by Captain Scott. He committed suicide rather than endanger his colleagues by slowing them down. Legend says that he walked out of his tent into the snowy wastes, saying: 'I am going out now. I may be some time.'

- **The legend of the *Mary Celeste*** tells of a ship found drifting in the Atlantic Ocean in December 1872. The last entry in the ship's log was 25 November. The entire crew had vanished without trace.

▲ *The Mary Celeste was a small trading vessel bound from New York for Genoa. Her crew mysteriously disappeared without any sign of violence or emergency.*

- ***The Ring***, a modern film based on the ancient Japanese tradition of ghost legends, tells how anyone who watches a strange videotape meets a mysterious death seven days later.

197

Defeating death

- **Christian stories** say that Jesus could raise people from the dead. He brought back to life one man, Lazarus, who had been in his tomb for four days.

- **Norse myth says** that when the god of light, Baldur, was killed, the goddess of death, Hela, said she would give him back his life if every living thing in the universe wept for him. All things wept except one – the evil god Loki.

- **The Khoi people of South Africa** tell a myth in which a man called Tsui'goab defeated Death in a wrestling match to save his village from perishing in a drought.

- **Greek myth says that the hero Heracles** once wrestled Death to win back the life of a woman called Alcestis, the wife of his friend King Admetus.

- **A Hindu myth** tells of how the Lord of Death had a child by a human woman, without telling the woman who he really was. When the child grew up, he blackmailed the Lord of Death into keeping alive a sick princess, by threatening to tell his mother the real identity of his father.

- **In Russian myth,** Koschchei is a wizard who cheats death by keeping his soul hidden inside an egg, inside a duck, inside a hare, inside an iron chest, under an oak tree, on an island in the middle of a wide ocean.

- **According to Greek myth**, an elderly couple called Philemon and Baucis were such good people that the gods granted them a wish – to die at the same time. The gods turned them into trees, which twined their branches around each other in an eternal embrace.

- **King Arthur's knights** were once challenged by a giant Green Knight to cut off his head. Sir Gawain bravely volunteered. However, the Green Knight just picked up his head and stuck it back on again!

● **An episode of the TV series *Charmed*** was based on the myth that cats have nine lives. A witch's cat found out how to turn himself into human form. Then he tried to get himself killed nine times to use up his cat's lives so he could remain human for ever.

▶ *In the Arthurian myth of Sir Gawain, the character of the Green Knight has its roots in traditional beliefs about a 'green man of the woods' – the spirit of nature which dies and is reborn each year.*

...FASCINATING FACT...
Siberian people believed that their holy men (or shamans) became even more powerful after death.

Ghosts and ghouls

- **The Japanese** believe that after death a soul is angry. They carry out rituals over seven years to purify it into a peaceful spirit – or it will return to the land of the living as a ghost.

- **The Maya** believed that each person was accompanied through life by a ghostly animal spirit called a nagual.

- **In Eastern European legends**, Rusalki were souls of unbaptized babies or drowned young girls who turned into river spirits.

- **A house in Amityville**, New York, was haunted by terrifying happenings after a man called Ronald Defeo shot his whole family there on 13 November 1974. The legend became known as the Amityville Horror.

- **A duppy is a West Indian ghost** believed to appear if you throw coins and a glass of rum onto its grave.

- **People in Eastern European countries** believed in ghosts called Wila – the restless spirits of dead young women who had lived frivolous lives.

◄ *Anne Boleyn was the second wife of Henry VIII, whom he had beheaded. It is said that her ghost haunts the Tower of London. Her daughter became Queen Elizabeth I, arguably the greatest queen of England.*

▶ The Legend
of Sleepy Hollow
*was made into a
Hollywood movie
in 1999, directed
by Tim Burton
and starring
Johnny Depp and
Christina Ricci.*

- *The Legend of Sleepy Hollow* tells of the terrifying ghost of a headless horseman. The American writer Washington Irving (1783–1832) wrote the story, based on a Dutch legend.

- **The Tower of London in England** is said to be haunted by the ghosts of many people who were imprisoned there. One is Anne Boleyn, a wife of Henry VIII whom he had beheaded.

- **Drifting gaseous flames** can sometimes be seen at night over marshy land. These were once thought to be the wandering ghosts of children, called 'will o' the wisps'.

- *The Flying Dutchman* is a ghost ship which is said to lure real ships into danger around the Cape of Good Hope at the southern tip of Africa.

201

Spirit journeys

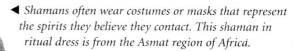

◄ *Shamans often wear costumes or masks that represent the spirits they believe they contact. This shaman in ritual dress is from the Asmat region of Africa.*

● **Many ancient tribal peoples** believed that their holy leaders, or 'shamans', could leave their bodies and journey through the spirit world.

● **Polynesian myth** tells that the dead walk down a path called Mahiki, through a seaside cave, to reach the world of spirits, Lua-o-Milu.

● **The Maya believed** that the road to the Underworld was steep and dangerous. It was covered with thorns and gushing torrents of water tried to sweep souls away into abysses on either side.

● **A story from the Book of Genesis** in the Bible tells that Jacob once saw angels going up and down a ladder between Earth and heaven.

● **According to Classical myth**, Charon was the ferryman who sailed souls to the Underworld.

● **Plains Native Americans** believed that souls had to cross a bridge to the afterlife guarded by an Owl Woman. She flung off unidentified souls into an abyss below.

● **Muslim stories say that Al Sirat** is the bridge to heaven. It is narrower than a spider's thread and sharper than a sword. Wicked souls fall off it and tumble down to hell.

● **Ancient Persian** stories say that the Chinvat bridge to heaven is guarded by an angel called Rashnu. He holds golden scales to weigh the souls of the dead.

● **The Ancient Egyptians** believed that souls travelled to the Underworld by boat, steered by a ferryman called Aken.

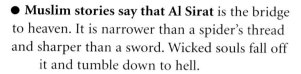

◀ *This kachina, or spirit figure, was made by the Hopi people of North America. The Hopi honour the spirits of the Sun, winds, rain and maize plants (their traditional staple food).*

......**FASCINATING FACT**....
The Incas believed that in order to reach paradise, Hanan Pacha, good souls had to cross a bridge woven from hairs.

203

Past and new lives

- **Voodoo myths in Africa and the Caribbean** tell of zombies – dead people who are brought back to life, but without minds or feelings.

- **Medieval Jewish legends** tell of rabbis who made golem – clay people who are brought to life by means of a charm to become zombie-like servants.

- **Hindu stories say that the god Vishnu** has appeared on Earth in nine incarnations to help humans. These nine forms are known as 'avatars'.

- **Hindus believe** that when a person dies, their soul moves on to a new life. If the person was good in their past life, their new life will be better. If the person was bad in their past life, they will be reincarnated into a harsh life of suffering.

- **According to Buddhist tradition**, a person who lives a selfish life wanting many things is likely to be born again as a hungry ghost called a preta, whose greed can never be satisfied.

- **For the Maya**, the sea-snail was a symbol of resurrection after death.

▲ *These Buddhist monks own very few possessions and live a very simple life of prayer. They believe that by doing so, they may achieve absolute peace and break out of the endless earthly cycle of death and reincarnation.*

- **Egyptian myth** says that the goddess Isis resurrected the murdered god Osiris by searching for the scattered pieces of his body and then restoring him to life by using the rites of embalment.

- **Heqt was the Egyptian goddess of** resurrection. She was pictured with the head of a frog.

- **Many modern plays and films** have been based on a mythical monster called Frankenstein who was created by a scientist from parts of dead human bodies and brought to life with the help of electricity. This myth in fact developed from the 1816 novel *Frankenstein* by Mary Shelley, in which Frankenstein was the name of the scientist, not the monster he created.

- **Due to advances** in genetic engineering, scientists now know in theory how to create a human being in the laboratory. The Frankenstein myth is close to becoming a reality.

▲ *In modern myth, Frankenstein is a hideous zombie-like monster who is created and brought to life by a mad scientist.*

Visions of the end

● **Stories about the end of the world** are said to be eschatological myths. Tales about the creation of the world are called cosmogonical.

● **In the Bible**, Saint John predicts that four mighty horsemen representing war, famine, plague and death will appear at the end of the world, with many other terrifying creatures.

● **The Fon tribe of Africa** believe that the world is circled by a huge sea snake. One day, he will no longer be able to support the Earth's weight and it will sink to the bottom of the ocean.

● **The Aztecs believed that at the end of the world**, their god Quetzalcoatl would return to them. When the Spaniards invaded in 1519, the Aztecs believed that the Spanish leader was the returning Quetzalcoatl and so allowed themselves to be conquered.

▲ *Islamic stories say that angels write down people's deeds, so God can judge them at the end of the world.*

● **Norse myth tells of Ragnarok**, which means 'the doom of the gods'. A huge battle will take place between the forces of evil and the forces of good – which evil will win. Then a new universe will be born.

● **Jewish mythology** tells of an angel called Israfel. He spends all eternity holding a trumpet to his lips, ready for God to tell him to announce the end of the world.

● **According to Persian myth,** the end of time will begin when a currently chained dragon, Azhi Dahaka, breaks free.

- **An Inca story** says that if mankind becomes too wicked, the god Viraccocha will weep a flood of tears which will sweep humans away.

- **According to Islamic myth**, every person has an angel who follows them all their lives and writes down everything they do – good and bad. At the end of the world, everyone will be judged by their book of deeds.

- **Many twentieth-century people** used to think that the human race would most likely be destroyed by nuclear war. Now people think we will be wiped out either by a deadly virus or a natural disaster such as a meteorite hitting the Earth.

◀ *Some scientists think that the dinosaurs may have been wiped out due to a meteorite or asteroid hitting Earth. Is this how the human race will also meet its end?*

Index

Index

Index

Index

Index

Index

Index

Acknowledgements

**The publishers would like to thank the following artists
who contributed to this book:**

Julie Banyard, C.M. Buzer (Luigi Galante Studio), Vanessa Card, Jim Channell,
Peter Dennis (Linda Rogers), Nicholas Forder, Chris Forsey, Terry Gabbey,
Luigi Galante (Luigi Galante Studio), Alan Hancocks, Sally Holmes, Richard Hook,
Rob Jakeway, John James (Temple Rogers), Barry Jones, Roger Kent, Stuart Lafford,
Priscilla Lamont, Kevin Maddison, M Mangeri (Luigi Galante Studio), Janos Marffy,
Tracey Morgan, Chris Odgers, Roger Payne, Rachel Phillips, Gill Platt, Terry Riley,
Martin Sanders, Peter Sarson, Susan Scott, Caroline Sharpe, Rob Sheffield,
Pam Smy, Roger Stewart, Gwen Tourret, Peter Utton, Rudi Vizi, Steve Weston,
Mike White (Temple Rogers), John Woodcock

**The publishers would like to thank the following sources
for the use of their photographs:**

39 The Art Archive; 61 Universal/Dreamworks/Scott Free/Pictorial Press;
71 The Art Archive/Archaeological Museum Aleppo Syria/Dagli Orti;
89 New Line Productions/Pictorial Press; 101 Margaret Courtney-Clarke/CORBIS;
108 RKO/Pictorial Press; 133 Warner Bros/Pictorial Press;
143 The Art Archive/Eileen Tweedy; 149 Fulvio Roiter/CORBIS;
155 TCF/Greenlawn/National Periodical Publications/Pictorial Press;
165 Historical Picture Archive/CORBIS; 201 Paramount/Mandalay/American
Zoetrope/Pictorial Press; 205 Universal/Pictorial Press

All other pictures from the Miles Kelly Archives

Corbis, Corel, digitalSTOCK, digitalvision, Dover, Hemera, ILN, PhotoAlto, PhotoDisc